A WESTERN

Trilogy

by Bill Pierce

TURNER PUBLISHING COMPANY
Publishers of America's History
412 Broadway•P.O. Box 3101
Paducah, Kentucky 42002-3101
(502) 443-0121

By: Bill Pierce

Publisher's Editor: Bill Schiller
Designer: David Hurst
Cover and Illustrations by Eve Bernard

Library of Congress Catalog No. 99-066917
ISBN 978-1-63026-933-3
LIMITED EDITION

Dedication

I dedicate this book to my wife who has been very helpful in providing a woman's point of view.

Contents

SWEET
REVENGE

HELL HATH NO FURY

H ugh Rexler rode cautiously down the thinly wooded slope, carefully scanning the grassy, open valley at the foot of the long hill. Being a wary man, he paused before leaving the sparse cover of the scrubby pines trees. Looking out from under the low brim of his low-crowned Stetson, his intense brown eyes looked nearly black.

It paid to be very careful in his line of work. Being a bounty hunter was rewarding but also dangerous. He had, of course, made enemies. The follower was also careful, but Hugh was aware that *someone* was following him from a distance. It could be another bounty hunter, or maybe just a fellow traveler. That was doubtful, though, as the person had been careful to stay out of his direct sight.

During the night, he had circled back to try and discover who it was, but he had been outsmarted; all he found was another set of horse tracks. He followed a short way but had lost the tracks in the darkness.

After looking over the lay of the valley, he quickly picked his way down the remaining slope and dashed for the cover of the trees at the other end of the valley. Once he reached the sheltering trees, he turned and looked back. There was no sign of the other rider. He stopped and uncorked his canteen.

From a safe distance, Francine Solon watched as the bounty hunter tipped back his Stetson and uncorked his canteen to drink deeply, his eyes closed. She could have shot him right then and had reached for her Winchester, half drawing it from its scabbard. Then she pushed it back into its sheath. She had every right to kill the man, but she wanted him to know who she was and why he was going to die.

He had shot down her husband of three weeks. Dear Charles, how she had loved him. And still, despite their three weeks of marriage, she knew so little about him save for the fact that he was a kind and gentle man.

Francine had felt so safe and warm in his arms as they shared intimate embraces. A tear trickled down her soft cheek as she thought of how his young life had been cut short. It appeared the hunter was heading for the next town. At least that was the direction. Should she ride ahead and get there first? What if that wasn't his destination and he just rode around the town? No, it was better to follow.

She had been following this man for nearly three weeks. Having buried her man, she was determined not to lose the opportunity to confront this beast and extract her revenge. His horse was an easy one to keep track of, as its brown hip had a distinct patch of white in the shape of a roughly off-center diamond.

Hugh still thought about the three-week-old event that kept him on the dodge. If wishes were pennies, beggars could ride, but wishing wasn't going to change any of the facts. He had killed a man. Now he was somewhere in the Dakota territories. His wanderings had taken him east and south from his hurried getaway point. He wasn't sure just where he was, but there appeared to be a town up ahead... maybe a mile or two. Surely, that would be a place where a man could get a drink and rest for a spell before going on.

He reached the edge of the small town and crossed the wooden wagon bridge that spanned the slow running creek. As he looked down the street, the false front stores and buildings were typical of the 1894 era: weathered and silvery gray from the harsh winters and the baking sun of summers.

He wanted to stable his tired horse, get him grain-fed and let him rest for a few days. Lord knows, the horse had faithfully carried him all these miles.

Getting his horse out of sight of whoever was following him was another plus. As the late afternoon sun's blaze began to mellow, Hugh rode up to the stable at the other end of town and dismounted. He led the horse to the watering trough and let him drink. As the horse drank, Hugh looked up and down the street. Although there were a few mounted men here, he had no clue as to which, if any, had been following him.

The hostler came out of the livery barn and hobbled toward the watering trough.

"Stable your horse, mister?"

Hugh looked up. *"Yes, and feed him some grain. I plan on staying in town a couple of days and nights."*

The hostler took the reins and turned to lead the horse inside.
Hugh took off his Stetson and dipped his head into the water trough. He came up for air shaking his head and blowing. Rubbing the water out of his eyes and using his hands to slick down his black hair, an idea struck him and he followed the hostler into the livery barn.

He sat down on a bale of hay and watched as the hostler stripped off the horses's saddle, saddlebags, and blanket. As the hostler placed the saddlebags on a sawhorse, Hugh stood and walked over there. He dug into his saddlebags and rummaged until he found the round tin of bootblack.

Hugh twisted off the lid and removed the piece of rag. He then rubbed the black dye into the white diamond-shaped spot on the horse's hip. This would serve to conceal the distinctive mark on the horse. It wouldn't withstand close inspection, but would serve to throw off a quick glance.

He walked to the Clearwater Saloon right across the street and pushed through the batwing doors. There were barback mirrors, an assortment of bottles, strategically placed coal oil lamps, deal tables neatly placed around the room, piano player busy with a tune. The bar was lined with an assortment of men, some in rough work clothes, some in business suits, and some cowboys. Two bartenders were busy serving drinks.

He found a place at the bar and when one of the busy bartenders paused in front of him, Hugh just nodded and said,

"Whiskey."

The bartender placed a clean glass in front of him and poured it nearly full to the brim. Hugh dug into his pocket and found a half-dollar which he dropped on the bartop. The bartender returned 40 cents change. Sipping his drink, Hugh continued to look carefully about the saloon.

Francine circled the town and entered from the opposite end. She checked each horse along the street. The brown one wasn't there. Had she misjudged this man? Had he ridden on through the town and then turned either east or west?

She turned back and saw the livery stable at the end of the street. That was it! She rode up to the watering trough and let her horse drink. She dismounted and noticed the hostler was in the haymow dropping fresh hay through the opening. She tied her horse to one of the stalls and walked along carefully looking at each horse. None had a white patch on its hip. As she stood wondering how she could have been mistaken, the hostler climbed down from the haymow.

"Ma'am? Do you wish to stable your horse?"

"Did someone ride in just recently and leave a brown horse here with a white diamond shape on its hip?"

The hostler looked at her closely. *"Why do you ask?"*

Francine tried to think of the best way to answer his question. Truth won out.

"That man is a bounty hunter and he shot down my husband. Error or not, I plan to do my best to kill that man."

The hostler looked startled. *"A bitty thing like you, ma'am, is gonna face down a man over a gun? I admire your spunk but don't hold much of a chance for you. On the other hand, if it's determined you are, that's his horse in the next-to-last stall. He done rubbed boot black on that white patch of hair."* The hostler pointed toward the stall on the left.

Francine examined the horse, paying particular attention to his left hip. There it was. The white patch had been blended in with the boot black, making it invisible at a quick glance. So, the man knew someone was on his trail, and she had been so careful to stay out of his sight. She had thought he doubled back the other night just to be sure, but hiding the white patch was proof that he knew.

She knew what he looked like, but her face was unknown to him. That gave her a slight advantage. In all probabilities, he would go to the nearest saloon to wash the trail dust out of his throat and then find a hotel room for overnight. That made it easy; there was only one hotel.

Francine paid the hostler to take care of her horse and walked to the hotel across the street. She carried her saddlebags over her arm as she checked into the hotel. Her room was hot and stuffy, so she opened the windows that faced the street and then unpacked her clothes from the saddlebags. Her blouse and skirt were badly wrinkled. She shook them out and draped them over the bedstead.

Francine poured the tepid water from the pitcher into the enamel basin and washed up as best she could. She felt more feminine after dressing in the skirt and blouse. The jeans and flannel shirt would serve for the trail, but were not at all ladylike attire. As she finished brushing her dark hair, she turned to glance out the window and saw the bounty hunter.

It was the man she had followed for weeks, heading for the hotel. This was luck, and she had guessed right. She quickly left her room, darted down the stairs and as she entered the lobby, she could see him scratching his name on the register. He finished, laid some coins on the desk, and turned toward the stairs. He glanced briefly at her and tipped his hat. She turned and waited, then followed him up the stairs.

Francine discovered his room was three doors down the hall from hers. Should she knock on his door and face him down? Maybe not. There was probably a better way. Using her feminine charm to put him off guard would, in all probability, be a more subtle action.

She reached into her skirt pocket and withdrew her two-shot, .41 caliber Derringer. She broke open the action to make sure both barrels were loaded. Satisfied, she slipped the gun back into her pocket and approached his door.

She rapped quietly and heard his footsteps approach. The

door opened a crack and he peered out with one eye. A look of wonder and puzzlement crossed his face as he swung the door open.

"Hello, may I come in?" Francine asked.

Hugh was more than puzzled. Nice girls don't just enter a man's hotel room without an invitation. On the other hand, this pretty lady didn't have her face painted up as a prostitute would. He stepped back and ushered her in.

As she entered the man's room, Francine noticed his gunbelt and six-gun were hanging from the bedstead. Her instincts told her that as careful as this man was, he wouldn't leave himself unprotected. In all probabilities, he was carrying a concealed gun somewhere on his person. As he followed her further into the room, Francine stopped, turned, drew her Derringer and pointed it at the man.

"Mister Rexler, does the name Solon mean anything to you? Please remove any concealed weapons you are carrying and place them on the washstand beside you."

Hugh bent and pulled a short-barreled pistol from his boot. His face took on an ashen look as he placed it on the washstand.

"You were his wife then?" He realized how badly he had misjudged the pretty face. *"How well did you really know Charles Solon?"*

Francine looked directly into the man's eyes. *"He was my husband of three weeks and I loved him. I knew him well enough to know how gentle and loving a man he was. You robbed us of our happiness and our life together. Now I am going to take your life as forfeit."* Her hand tightened on the grip of her gun. *"Do you have any last words before you meet my justice?"*

"So you are prepared to be the judge, jury, and executioner, without even giving me a trial?"

"What kind of a trial did my husband have? You executed him without a trial." Francine retorted.

Hugh shifted his weight from one leg to the other. *"I gave him every chance to surrender, but he went for his gun and I had no choice."*

"So then you took the law into your own hands and shot him down." Her eyes were sharp and angry looking.

Hugh could tell she was ready to pull the trigger. *"May I show you something before you pull that trigger, ma'am?"*

"What could you show me that would make any difference?"

"If you just open my saddlebag there, you'll find a reward poster with the name of Charles Solon and a very good likeness of your husband on it."

Disbelief clouded Francine's face. Was this some kind of a trick? She watched him very closely as she reached into the saddle-bags and rummaged around without taking her eyes off him. Her searching fingers found a folded piece of paper and withdrew it. Still keeping her eyes on Hugh, she unfolded the poster. A quick glance at it and there indeed was Charles staring back at her. Her heart gave a lurch as she read,

"Wanted, dead or alive, for the torture, battery, and murder of 9 young women. Reward $1,000."

"I believe, ma'am, that you would have been his tenth victim."

How could this be? Francine wondered. He had been so loving and tender. There must be some mistake. Could this be true? There was the inheritance she had never touched. It wasn't much and Charles had never mentioned it after she told him about it. Could this be her Charles? It was difficult to understand, and her mind was in a turmoil.

Hugh had edged closer to the woman. He could see she was in a state of confusion and denial. The Derringer, clenched in her delicate hand, was cocked and still pointed in his direction. He watched as she studied the likeness on the reward poster and read the words again. Hugh really looked at her. More than just a glance. He studied the shape of her face. She wasn't a beautiful woman, but not homely by any means. Her eyes were strikingly green, which he thought was unusual with her dark hair. She was rather a small woman, but very nicely formed. If her mouth hadn't been drawn down into a frown, she would look much prettier, he thought. At the moment, she looked confused. Was he close enough to slap the gun out of her hand? He didn't think so.

Francine then noticed how close the man had gotten and took a step back.

"Don't do that again. I haven't decided just yet what to do with you. This poster has given me so much to think about and I need time to really mull this all over. I am going to carefully put this Derringer on half-cock so it won't accidentally go off, but don't you move, or even think I have made any decision." She still looked very grim.

Hugh shifted his weight and cleared his throat. This was a plus in his favor. He watched as she let down the hammers of the cocked gun.

"Ma'am, I'm sure the sheriff, or a town marshal here could show you the same reward poster. Another fact is this situation, why did Charles go for his six-shooter if he had been innocent of these brutal crimes? He knew his career of savage actions, with no mercy in his heart for his victims, was over when I faced him. I could see the cruelty in his eyes."

Francine listened to what the man was saying and had to agree with some of what he said, but still the memory of her husband's tender affection toward her and the gentle way he had held her, made it difficult to believe Charles could be so cruel and brutal. She made a decision.

"Mr. Rexler, we are going to pay a visit to the law officer of this small town and if indeed he can show me this same poster, then I will consider what you have told me." She wasn't totally convinced that this wasn't just a ploy, but would give the man the benefit of

doubt until she could be sure. Again she remembered Charle's soft caress and the tenderness of his lovemaking as they had shared the intimacy of their marriage bed. This was something that was burned in her memory and would never leave. How could she be so wrong about the man she loved?

Hugh relaxed just a bit as he could see she was beginning to consider all he had said and shown her. He watched as she slipped the gun into the pocket of her skirt.

"Just remember I have this gun in my pocket and will not hesitate to use it. Now, let's walk down the stairs and see if we can find the marshal's office."

He led the way as they left the room and stepped down the stairway. The lobby was empty except for the dozing hotel clerk. Of course, it was suppertime and most were enjoying the evening repast. On the boardwalk, Hugh paused and looked both directions up and down the street. The days light was fading and he almost missed the hand lettered sign with a six-point star below the legend, "Marshal."

Hugh nodded toward the sign across the street. *"There it is, ma'am."* Both of them stepped off the boardwalk and crossed the deserted street. As they reached the other side, Hugh stamped his feet to shake off the excess dust. The office was squeezed between a gunsmith shop and a general store. As they entered the doorway, they could see two barred jail cells in back and the deserted chair behind the small desk.

"Hello?" Francine called.

"Howdy, folks." The voice was behind them. *"I saw you come in and was just down the street. What may I do for you?"*

Hugh waited to see if the lady would speak.

"Marshal, may I see the reward posters you have?"

"Certainly, ma'am." The marshal sat at his desk and opened a drawer. He rummaged through it and then laid a small pile of folded posters on his desk. *"And who would you be interested in?"*

Francine looked at Hugh and spoke, *"Do you have one there for Charles Solon?"*

"Solon? let me see here." He began to thumb through the pile of reward posters. As he turned the last poster he answered, *"No, I don't see one for Charles Solon."* The marshal scratched his head. *"Hmmm, I do seem to remember something about Solon though, but it has slipped my mind."*

Francine stared sharply at Hugh, a look of doubt crossing her comely features.

"Marshal", Hugh pleaded, *"will you please look in your drawer again. My life may depend on it."*

After a curious glance at Hugh, the marshal pulled the drawer open further and bent to look. *"Wait, here's another."* He unfolded the creased paper and there was Charles Solon's likeness. *"Hmmm a thousand dollar reward dead or alive for him. Say, he is a bad one, isn't he?"*

Francine held out her hand. *"Please, let me see that, marshal."* The marshal looked up and handed her the poster.

She stared at the poster. A look of sadness crept into her eyes. *"He was my husband for three weeks and I loved him with all my heart. Now, I find I could have been his tenth victim. What kind of a twisted mind could conceive that type of brutal savagery? I would have gladly given him what money I had and I would imagine those other girls would have too. Why, oh why did God put inhumane beasts like him on this earth?"* Francine folded the poster and dropped it on the marshal's desk. *"You can toss this one away. Charles Solon is dead."* She wiped a tear from her eye.

Hugh understood how she felt. The pain of losing a loved

one, but also the terror of realizing how she could have ended up as his next victim. He stepped beside her and put his arm around her.

Without thought she laid her head on his shoulder. Her thoughts were in a turmoil. This man had killed her husband, but had also saved her from a horrible fate. On the other hand, could it be that Charles had put it all behind himself and had decided to settle down with her for a lifetime? This was something she would never know for sure. The fact was Charles was gone in any case. Here was his killer offering her sympathy and a shoulder to lean on. Something stirred in her breast. Was she transferring her feelings from Charles to Hugh Rexler? She knew he was sympathetic and in her present mood she needed someone to cling to.

The marshal cleared his throat and said, *"Well, folks, I'm going to supper. You stay here if it pleases you."* He stood and walked out the door.

Francine turned to face Hugh, put her arms around him and wept with her head pressed against his chest. *"Why"*, she asked, *"does life have to be so confusing?"*

Hugh held her tenderly not knowing how to answer her and also grateful 'e didn't put two bullet holes in his head when she first came into his room. He couldn't help but feel some affection for this young woman and holding her close like this was affecting him more than he wanted to admit.

"Mr. Rexler, would you just hold me like this, for a short spell, and then take me to supper? I need to feel there is someone in this world who cares." She murmured against his chest.

"Only on one condition, Ma'am."

"Please, call me Francine."

Hugh laughed out loud.

"You're laughing at me."

"I laughed because I was about to ask you to call me Hugh." He took her hand and led her toward the door.

Francine took a handkerchief from her blouse and wiped her eyes. Hugh tucked her hand under his elbow and they both left the marshal's office. They paused outside and both looked up and down the street and Francine pointed to a sign which read "The Boardinghouse Restaurant."

"There, that seems to be the only place in town to get anything to eat. I'm tired of trail food and lonely campfires."

"Francine, I agree. Let's go over there and demolish whatever they are serving!" Hugh smiled. They crossed the street pausing only to let a team of horses, pulling a loaded wagon, go by.

The restaurant was crowded as Hugh removed his Stetson and looked for a table. The only one he could see that might be a possibility, was occupied by the town marshal who was wolfing down his meal. Hugh steered Francine to that table and when the marshal looked up, he asked, *"Marshal, do you mind if we join you?"*

The marshal stood quickly, nearly spilling his coffee.

"Sir and ma'am, be my guest." He remained standing as Hugh pulled out a chair and seated Francine.

Francine was trying to sort out her thoughts. She wondered why she felt as she did about Hugh Rexler. At first she wanted to gun him down, but after discovering what sort of man she had chosen for a husband and finding out about his brutal career, it left her confused. Fate had a way of upsetting a persons plans and lifestyle. Now, here she was feeling grateful and attracted to Hugh Rexler, her husband's killer. How could she have been so mistaken?

Hugh could see the lady was in a turmoil. He was relieved that she had decided not to gun him down and he discovered she was attracted to him. Could it be sympathy? He didn't think so. Other young women were interesting, but there was a connection here he didn't understand. As he studied the menu, printed in chalk on the blackboard, his mind began to wander and a fantasy formed in his imagination. He was holding the lovely girl in his arms and he could feel the softness and warmth radiate from her. He looked down and studied her face. . .the way her dark hair fell across one eyebrow, how her straight nose turned up at the end, the sparkle in her green eyes, the way her full lips looked when she smiled and a pretty smile it was. He wanted to hold her tight and kiss those full lips...

"Mister Rexler?" The daydream ended.

"Yes, Ma'am?" he answered and turned to face her.

"I asked what you were having for supper?"

"Well now, the beefsteak and fried taters look mighty tempting. Maybe apple pie for desert." He answered.

"I think I am going to order the sugar cured ham with gravy and biscuits." Francine answered.

She studied his face as he looked about the room. Not dazzlingly handsome, but he had craggy looks. His black hair was unruly and his nose had been broken, but it gave his face character. When he had put his arms around her, it was as though a current ran through her. There was magic in his touch and it was something she had never before felt in her young life. She wondered how he felt about her, *really*.

The marshal finished his coffee and stood. *"Well, folks, I'm taking my leave."* He turned and left the restaurant.

Surprise was her reaction as Hugh took her soft hand in his rough work worn, but gentle grip. There was that feeling of closeness and yearning that ran through her body again.

"Francine, I can't help myself. I'm strongly attracted to you." He seemed shy and hesitant.

"Oh, Hugh, do you feel it too? It's like a strong current running through me." She shuddered. As if by a common signal they both stood and clasped each other. Hugh kissed her deeply and tightened his arms. Francine felt dizzy, but extremely happy. It was exciting and just felt so right. A bond between them had formed. Francine hoped, with all her heart, it would last.

Their food arrived and they both sat down to enjoy it. Hugh tasted his beefsteak. He wondered how things had come to pass. First, Francine had been hunting him down and now they were on the brink of falling in love. Strange how Cupid's arrows seemed to find their mark in the most impossible of situations. Her green eyes really seemed to go with Francine's personality.

As she cut her ham into little pieces she glanced shyly at Hugh. It seemed the more she saw of him, the more he appealed to her. She blushed as she daydreamed about lying wrapped in his arms in a feather bed. Her mind savored that thought, but refused to carry it any further. Maybe it was just as well to keep it in the back of her mind and anticipate the reality of it instead of just fantisizing.

Hugh had the feeling she was watching him and glanced her way. Her hair had fallen across one of her eyes and strangely it made her look more vulnerable. He wondered if there really was a possibility of a lasting romance in their future.

"Francine?"

She put her fork down and smiled. "Yes?"

"I was just wondering if there could be romance in our near future?" There! He had blurted out what his heart was yearning for.

Francine was cautious, but her heart was beating at a faster pace and she suddenly felt warm all over. Her answer was on the tip of her tongue, but she held back. Was this what she really wanted, or was it just her feeling of lonesomeness and being wanted by someone? Her short marriage had just whetted her appetite for the closeness and loving feelings she had longed for as a girl. Would this be her last chance, or would someone else come along? Hugh, as he had held her, had caused feelings she had never experienced before and she yearned to feel that way again. She made up her mind.

"Yes, Hugh, there is a very good chance we can become closer."

He seemed to have been holding his breath, waiting for her answer. He, too, had felt the rush as he held and kissed her. This was something he wanted to feel over and over again.

"Francine, I'm beginning to fall in love with you, and hope you feel the same way." He was serious.

She looked deep into his eyes and was stirred to her very soul. They had more or less chosen each other and found what a thrill just standing close with their arms about each other could be. Now, could she disuade him from his bounty hunting career? Or was it too early to bring up that subject. It would be better to wait.

"Hugh, I'm going back to my hotel room and relax a bit. I am really saddle weary from keeping up on the trail." She stood and they both left.

She tucked her hand into the crook of his arm and they crossed the dusty street again. Hugh felt the occasional bump from her hip as they walked together and his thoughts turned to a feeling of intimatacy. He wondered if she would respond to his advances.

Francine had purposely bumped him with her hip and wondered if she would have to take the initiative and make the first advance. The heat in her loins had been building and relief was right here beside her. She decided to be aggressive and would go to his room after the hotel was all quiet. She noticed how he kept glancing at her and she believed he would be receptive to it.

"Thank you, Hugh, for the evening supper and also for the companionship." She gave his arm a squeeze.

"It was my pleasure, Francine." He answered.

She climbed the stairs and went into her room. Jumping back in shock and letting a gasp of surprise escape her lips. She discovered someone had gone through her saddlebags and her personal effects were scattered on the floor.

Chapter 2

Hugh climbed the steps shortly after Francine had disappeared at the head of the stairs. As he walked quietly down the short hall, he heard Francine's gasp and quietly tapped on her door. The door was flung open nearly catching him unawares. Francine looked angry and at the same time fearful.

"What is it, Francine?" His eyes darted about the room.

"Just look. Somebody has gone through my things and strewn them all over the floor. Who and why?" She was mystified.

"The why of it is evident. They were looking for something," Hugh answered. *"Is there anything missing?"*

Francine turned and took inventory. "Nothing that I know of is missing. . .wait! My mother's broach is gone! That broach had mom and dad's pictures in it and it's all I have left to remember them by. The cost isn't an issue, but it has great sentimental value to me."

"Francine, I'm sorry you lost your treasure. If there was a way to replace it, I would." Hugh told her.

"You better check your room and see if its been robbed too."

Hugh looked startled, he hadn't even thought about his room. He turned and left through the open door. He wondered what he'd find. He opened his room door and found none of his belongings had been disturbed. His Colt and gun belt were still draped on the bedstead, the hideout gun was on the washstand and his saddlebags hadn't been disturbed. This was strange. Three doors away, Francine's room had been gone through, but not his. He pondered on that.

He stripped off his shirt and poured water into the wash basin. He bathed as best he could with the cold water and then rinsed off. His bed looked mighty inviting after his long ride and just a blanket by a campfire wasn't the best way to get a good night's sleep. Feeling for the coverlet and turning it down, he crawled into bed. He hoped he could get a restful night's sleep. As he lay staring at the dark ceiling, his thoughts turned to Francine.

He mentally reviewed her physical attributes. The soft dark brown hair and the ringlet that fell over one of her green eyes. Her eyebrows were darker than her hair. He remembered the lines of her face, oval in shape. The way her straight nose turned up at one end. Mostly he remembered the softness of her body as he had held her. The taste of her lips as they had kissed. Her breasts were petite as was the rest of her body. She had a flat stomach and he admired the way her hips flared from her waist. Soft and round. Imagining what her body would look like unclothed had him aroused and the frustration of just lying there thinking about what a joy it would be to join her caused a moan to escape him.

The doorknob of his door softly turned. As the door was quietly pushed open, it was difficult to tell in the dark, who was there. Merely a shadow deeper black than the night. He could imagine Francine standing in his doorway and feeling with her bare feet for objects on the floor so as not to stumble. The shadow did indeed make its way toward his bedside.

Hugh quivered with anticipation as the shadow neared. He heard the soft rustle of clothing drop and held back the coverlet to welcome Francine into his bed. She was completely nude as she snuggled her warm body against him.

It was a dream come true as Hugh enfolded her in his arms and there was that electric feeling of skin to skin contact. He tenderly kissed her and moved his hand caressing her rounded hip. Well, she had made the first move and seemed ready for more than just a casual relationship. This had all happened so quickly it gave him cause to wonder. Was this a dream, or was it really happening?

The doornob turned and the door began to open. All thoughts of romance were forgotten as Hugh reached for and grasped his Colt revolver. He disengaged himself from Francine's arms and waited. A darker shadow made its way toward them. As the shadow reached to open his saddlebags, laying on the floor beside the bed, Hugh took his heavy revolver and brought it crashing down on the prowler's head.

Without so much as a groan the body fell to the floor.

"Hugh, what is that?" Francine gasped.

"I believe we have found our sneak thief. Give me a moment to pull my trousers on and strike a light." Hugh arose from the bed and felt for his trousers. He quickly slipped them on and pulled a match from his pocket. Striking the match with his thumbnail, the feeble flame was like a torch in the darkness. Hugh turned the man over. A bag was loosley held in his hand. Hugh stood and lit the coal oil lamp. He took the bag from the man's limp fingers and dumped the contents of the bag on the bed. There were rings, pocket watches, money and other jewelry which included a pearl necklace, two sets of diamond earrings, a man's money belt and a ruby stickpin. There were also two broaches.

"Francine, is one of these broaches yours?"

She sat up modestly wrapped in the sheet and stared at the pile of loot. There was mother's broach! She reached for it and opened the catch. There were mom and dad's photos on tintype.

"You did find a way to get my treasure back, Hugh, and for that I am eternally grateful."

"I'm going down and get the room clerk. If this sneak thief even wiggles, take my gun and gut shoot the miserable little rat."

"Wait a moment and let me dress and go back to my own room. Hugh, please turn your back." She was suddenly modest.

He abided by her wishes and stared at the wall, hearing her hop from the bed and dress. Hearing the door open and close he turned around and stared at the unconcious man on the floor. He showed no signs of coming to.

Hugh left the room and stepped down the stairs. The room clerk slept with his head on folded arms resting on his desk. Hugh shook the man awake.

"What is it?" The clerk mumbled as his eyes fluttered open.

"I've caught a sneak thief in my room and did my best to bend my six-gun over his head. He has a bag full of loot. I want you to take charge while I go get the town marshal."

The room clerk, now awake sat up straight. *"You've caught him? Good! He's been a thorn in our side and we haven't been able to trap him."*

Funny, Hugh thought, the man should use the term 'trap' as the little man did resemble a mouse. He led the way and the clerk followed him up the stairs. As they entered the room, the clerk's nose detected the scent of woman. Well, so what? The man had done him a big favor catching the sneak thief. Fine and dandy, let the chips fall as they may.

The thief sat up with a groan and was rubbing the swelling lump on his head.

"Thick skulled little varmint, ain't you?" Hugh grinned. The blow would have felled an ox and crushed the skull of a lesser man. *"Here, clerk, take my gun and I'll go get the marshal. If he tries to stand up, gut shoot him."* Hugh handed his Colt .45 to the clerk and left the room.

"So, the rat is finally caught. Got too careless didn't you?" The clerk gloated, *"I, for one, am very glad. Now I won't have to hear our patron's complaints. Maybe I should just rap you on the skull again for all the trouble you've caused me."* The clerk grinned evilly and raised the heavy gun. The sneak thief didn't answer. He just stared sullenly at the clerk and continued to rub his head.

The clerk smiled and decided to take the credit for catching the thief. Now, maybe he could get the daytime job and let somebody else do the night work.

Hugh entered the marshal's office and found the man sleeping on one of the cots in a cell. *"Marshal?"* he called.

The man snorted and rolled over on his side. *"Who is it and what do you want?"*

"I have a room in the hotel and have caught a sneak thief in my room with a bag full of loot."

"You've caught him? Great!" The marshal sat up and rubbed his sleepy eyes. *"I'll come along and take charge of him."* He reached for his boots and pulled them on. Following Hugh, the marshal chuckled to himself. He would take credit for catching the sneak thief and maybe get the town fathers to cough up a little more cash for his monthly pay.

As they neared the hotel, they heard two shots fired. Both men broke into a lope and raced up the hotel stairs. Guests in various stages of undress were coming out their doors to see what was going on. The door to Hugh's room stood open. Hugh let the marshal, who was armed, enter the room first. The sneak thief lay dead on the floor and the clerk stood over him. *"He tried to jump me and I had no choice but to shoot him."* He explained.

Hugh looked at the loot laying on the bed and noticed the ruby stickpin and the money belt were missing. Glancing at the marshal he could see suspicion clouding his face, too. It seemed the room clerk had helped himself to some of the loot. He was undecided as to what to do. It was morally wrong for the thief to steal from the guests. It was just as wrong for the clerk to steal from the thief. Should he say anything to the marshal? The problem of indecision was solved for him.

"Bert, carefully lay that gun on the bed," the marshal ordered, placing his hand on his gun.

Bert nearly made a fatal decision. Hugh watched his hand tighten on the gun as through he would swing it around and end the marshal's life. He apparently thought the best of it and carefully laid the gun on the bed.

"That's the right move, Bert. I didn't want to have to shoot you down. You took some of the jewelry, didn't you?"

Bert was embarassed. *"Well, Marshal, you know what a poor living room clerks make. Really, the thief tried to jump me,"* he said with downcast eyes.

"Bert, I'm giving you the benefit of the doubt on that one," the marshal replied. *"Just put everything back on the bed."*

Bert dropped the stickpin and the money belt alongside the rest of the loot. The marshal turned to Hugh with a questioning look. Hugh just nodded.

"Well, I will take charge of this jewelry and in the morning try to get it back to the rightful owners." He picked each piece up and put it in the bag. *"Bert, help me carry this sneak thief's body out here."*

Bert reluctantly picked up the dead man's legs and the marshal got his hands under the shoulders. *"Mister,"* the room clerk gasped, *"soon as I get back I'm going to give you a different room, so's we can get this one cleaned up."*

Hugh dressed and pulled on his boots. He started at the blood on the worn carpet. So ended a man's life with probably no one to mourn him. He gathered up his saddlebags and slipped the spare short-barreled gun into his boot. He took one more glance about the room and then blew out the coal oil lamp. He left to wait in the lobby.

Francine had heard the shots and believed they had come from Hugh's room. Her heart gave a leap and began to race. Was Hugh still in there? She eased her door open and stared down the hall. Others were appearing at their doors and wondering what was going on. Just then the town marshal loped by, closely followed by Hugh.

The relief was so great, Francine felt her knees buckle and she caught herself on the door frame to keep from falling. The close contact with Hugh had affected her more than she wanted to admit. As he had taken her in his arms and their bodies had come together, the thrilling feeling of it was like a mild electric shock. She had been anticipating more, but then the sneak thief had come through the door. Disappointment had dampened the basic urge she had felt and she hoped to recapture that feeling again soon.

The room clerk and the town marshal had carried out the body of the thief, but then Hugh had left too and that caused her to wonder. She slipped out her door and walked down to Hugh's room. The room was dark, but the smell of blood answered her question. The clerk was going to give Hugh another room.

She returned to her room and waited. Soon she heard footsteps and peeked out to see Hugh, his saddlebags across his arm, open the door directly across from her room.

Francine smiled and made plans. She wanted to experience that exquisite feeling again. The feeling of being held in his embrace and being tenderly kissed.

Hugh dropped his saddlebags on the floor and sighed. Taking his watch out of his pocket, he discovered it was 1:45. Should he boldly go to her room, or wait to see if she was wiling to come to him? But, did she know he had been moved to a different room? Probably not, so he blew out the lamp and began to undress. The doorknob turned with a squeak and the door began to open.

"Francine?" He peered into the deep shadows.

"Why no, it's Jenny Lind, the Swedish Nightengale, come to sing you a lullaby."

Hugh sat on the edge of the bed and finished undressing. The lady had a sense of humor too. As he dropped his underwear on the floor and rolled across the bed, Francine joined him and cuddled close. Hugh once again took her in his arms and kissed her. Just lying there in each other's arms soon built the fires of passion. Both partners wanted more.

"Fire!" The cry startled both of them. *"The hotel's on fire!"* They both leapt from the bed and frantically scrambled to find their clothes in the dark. There was smoke and the crackle of burning wood. The cry was taken up by more and more people. Hugh and Francine quickly dressed and opened the door. The flames were racing up the stairway.

"*Come on!*" Francine cried, taking Hugh's hand, "*my room has a window in it!*"

He grabbed his saddlebags and followed her through the blinding smoke and to her room. Hugh stopped a second to slam the door behind them. They rushed to the open window and found lady luck had smiled. The roof over the verandah was only five feet below them. Hugh tossed both his and Francine's saddlebags onto the roof and they crawled out the window and dropped down. Now they had only to find their way to the ground.

Hugh peered over the edge and dropped both saddlebags. It was ten feet down.

"*Francine, I'm going to hang on to the eave and drop to the ground. Then you do the same and I'll catch you.*" He looked at her terrified face. "*It will be all right.*"

He crawled to the edge and let himself down. He clung to the eave for a second and then dropped. He landed on his feet and looked back up to see Francine's frightened face from the reflected glow of the fire, which seemed to be out of control.

She lowered herself over the edge of the roof and hung there fearfully. Finally her strength gave out and she let go. Hugh caught her, but they both tumbled to the dust of the street.

"*That was a close call, Hugh. I fear there will be some who won't be able to get out.*"

Francine was shivering from fear. A bucket brigade had formed, but it was useless. The fire had too good a start. They gave up trying to save the hotel and were tossing water on the surrounding buildings.

The saddle and harness shop next to the hotel was afire, and the air was filled with burning embers and sparks. The stable was just down the street.

"*Francine, I suggest we hightail it to the livery stable and saddle our horses. It appears to me this whole town is doomed. It looks like another campout under the stars for us, and it seems to me that will be better than an all over hot foot.*"

"My thoughts exactly. Those burning embers are heading right for the livery barn."

They both walked swiftly to the livery barn. As they arrived, the hostler was leading two horses out the front entrance and toward the creek. They entered the stable and Hugh quickly saddled both their horses and led them out.

"Here Francine, you hold our mounts. I'm going to help the hostler get the rest of these horses out."

Hugh dashed back into the building and gathered the reins of two more horses. He led them to the creek where the hostler had tied the other horses to some of the stronger willows that lined the bank. As he turned back, he could see the roof of the livery barn was beginning to blaze. He hurried back and plunged into the livery. The hostler was leading two more horses out and just nodded at Hugh. There was one horse still in a stall. It rolled its eyes in fear.

Hugh took off his shirt and wrapped it about the horse's head so that it couldn't see the flames. He led the frightened horse out of the building just as burning hay began to drop from the mow. As he led the horse outside, he met the hostler rushing back inside.

"This is the last horse. Don't go back in there!"

The hostler just glanced at Hugh. *"Mister, I ain't got no choice. My life savings is in there!"*

Was anyone's life savings worth a life? Hugh wondered. He glanced at the roaring flames and made a quick decision. There was no way he was reentering that inferno. It was a wise choice, as the whole roof collapsed in a shower of burning wood and sparks. He felt sorry for the man, but thought there was hope. The hostler ran from the flames carrying a carpetbag, his eyes wide with terror. His clothes were smoking and most of his hair was singed off. It was amazing he had been spared and with his life savings intact. The hostler turned and watched, with tears in his eyes, as the barn burned to the ground.

Hugh looked for Francine and found her at the edge of the

creek, holding the reins of both horses. He turned and looked back toward the main street of the town. He'd been right, the entire town was ablaze.

"Hugh, I worried as you entered that stable for the last time." Francine shuddered while reaching out to hug Hugh.

They mounted their horses and left the burning town. Traveling south at a leisurely pace, they rode for fifteen minutes before looking back. What was left of the town was a bright glow on the horizon.

"Have you noticed, every time we hold each other close, we are interrupted by a crisis? Is the Good Lord trying to tell us something?" Francine mused.

Hugh smiled and replied, *"I think it's just a coincidence and I'm going to prove it to you. See that grove of trees just ahead? Let's spread the bedrolls under them and put that rumor to rest."*

He turned toward Francine and she was laughing. *"I want nothing more than to feel your strong arms about me as you press your lips to mine."*

She urged her horse to a gallop. Surprised, Hugh followed at a slower lope. It seemed to him Francine was more eager than he thought. The thought of joining her under the stars was something he anticipated with great enthusiasm. When he reached the grove of trees, Francine had already tied her horse and was spreading her bedroll under a large elm tree. Hugh tied his horse to a small sapling, untied his bedroll and dropped it to the ground. The full moon was low in the sky and he glanced to where Francine was standing. The moon behind her was highlighting her hair, and she appeared to be wearing a halo.

He was mesmerized by the sight. A sense of longing overcame him. He wanted this woman now, but he also wanted to continue a relationship and finally make her his wife for the rest of his life. He was awestruck at how his thoughts had been turned in this direction. Hadn't he always been a drifter with the urge to see what was just over the next hill?

He unrolled his blankets right beside hers and hurriedly shed his clothes. Enfolding her soft warm body in his embrace, he held her tight as he kissed her sweet lips. As if by natural urge, they sunk down on the blankets. As he caressed her, she eagerly slid under him.

Suddenly both horses whinnied. Hugh heard the sound of an answering whinny and hoof beats thumping the ground. He sat up.

"Francine, it just isn't meant to be. Dress quickly and I will see what is going on."

Disappointment and frustration angered Francine as she quickly donned her clothes. She watched as Hugh dressed and strapped on his gunbelt. Oh, how she wanted to be intimate with this man, and she wanted him now. Hoping also for a future with him, but every time they became close, there was some kind of interruption. *Now what?*

She went over to stand by her horse. She watched as Hugh walked to meet whoever was coming at a full gallop. There were two horsemen and they slid to a halt just inside the grove.

"Listen, Hank, we was lucky this time, but sooner or later some sheriff and his posse is going to catch up with us. Are you hurt bad?"

Hank answered, *"I done lost alota blood and I'm getting weak. Can we start a fire? Are we far enough away from Highmore to risk it, Roy?"*

"We've got to risk it and stop that bleeding. Those towns-people were very upset at losing all their savings. I never heard so many shots fired at us. It sounded like the Civil War had started all over again! I was lucky to be missed with so much lead flying."

The men tied their horses and began to look for wood. Francine was sure her horse would whinny and let the men know there was someone else here. Was she far enough away to quietly lead their horses to the other edge of the grove? They would have to leave their bedrolls and quietly slip away in the dark. Hugh was nowhere to be seen, but she was sure he was watching the outlaws with an eagle eye. She decided to chance it and carefully led both horses away from the area where the men were looking for wood. Luck stayed with her until one of the two horses stepped on a dead branch.

"Is that you, Hank?"

"What?"

"What was that noise? It came from over there . . . Hey! Here's somebody's blankets. Hank, there's somebody else here! We've got to kill them!" Roy shouted.

"Don't be too hasty. If they were a threat they would have already challenged us."

"Think about it Hank. They have probably heard what we said and if they don't try to take our loot they will at least let the sheriff know which direction we took."

Francine was undecided. She didn't want to move, but the voices were close and coming her way. Where was Hugh? Should she leap on her horse and gallop away with both horses? Then she heard Hugh shout *"Gee up!"* and the sound of horses galloping away.

"Roy! There go our horses and loot! Come on!"

Francine heard both men crashing through the underbrush toward where they had left their mounts. Hugh had untied their horses and sent them galloping away. He waited until both men rushed to where they had left their horses tied. He held the lasso he'd found on one of the horses. As the men neared him, he calmly spoke.

"Alright, you rannies, your horses are gone. You have two choices. Start walking after them or take a chance on winging me."

Three shots rang out. The men had shot at where the voice was coming from. Hugh had played this game before. He had called out from behind a sturdy oak tree. Silence, as Hugh held his breath.

"Did we get him?"

"He didn't shoot back, we must have, but be very careful."

They crept toward where they had fired. Hugh waited in silence until he could see a shadowy form approach his place by the tree. He raised his Colt and crashed it down on the unsuspecting man's head.

"Roy?" the other outlaw called.

Hugh smiled and thought, *"These guys were on the lower end of the smarts chart. Just about as much sense as a sack of dried beans."*

The other shadowy form appeared close to the tree and Hugh again raised his Colt to crash it down on the man's head. Something warned him and he fired at Hugh. Hugh had no choice; he shot and killed the man. Hugh bound up the man who was unconscious with the lasso. Francine feared the worst. Five shots she had heard, three nearly together and then two more. In her mind she tried to think of what it meant. Was Hugh all right, wounded, dead, or had he prevailed? The outlaws had made as much noise as a rutting moose, crashing through the brush. Surely Hugh had heard them coming. Probably the four shots had been aimed at Hugh. To her the fifth shot had sounded different somehow. It could have been Hugh's gun. Still undecided, she waited, holding the reins of both horses.

"Francine?" It was Hugh's low-voiced call. Relief spread through her tense body.

"Over here, Hugh. I was leading both horses to the edge of the trees. I heard them when they found our blankets. I would have made it too, but one of the horses stepped on a dry stick and gave me away."

"You did the right thing and were out of the line of fire. I had to kill one of those men; he gave me no choice. The other is still unconscious. Let's gather up our bedding and get out of here. I won-

der if we should catch their horses and check on their loot?"

"Did you disarm both of them?"

"I tossed their guns deep into the woods. By the time the one comes to, we will be long gone from this place. As far as the dead one is concerned, let the buzzards have a meal."

Hugh appeared beside her and gave her a hug. *"Do you remember where our blankets are?"*

"Yes I do. I counted footsteps and I'm sure I can find them again."

Francine tied the reins to a sapling and they both backtracked to where the blankets were. They quickly rolled and tied their blankets, and mounted their horses. Hugh led the way south as they loped away. They rode side by side, without talking, each with their own thoughts. Francine was thinking about the warm protected feeling as Hugh had held her close. Would they ever get a chance to share what they both desired?

Hugh was worrying about the man he'd knocked unconscious. Had he hit him hard enough to kill him? He didn't think so. Would the man survive? Probably, as he was a rough-and-tough outlaw a wee bit short in the mental department. He might, after searching, find his gun that Hugh had thrown into the deeper woods.

As they loped along, both noticed the eastern horizon beginning to lighten. Soon it was light enough to see ahead, and off to the west there were two horses saddled and bridled, grazing on the sparse grass. In all probability, they belonged to the outlaws. Hugh turned and rode toward them and Francine followed. He caught up the reins of both horses and then dismounted to look in the saddlebags. They were stuffed with greenbacks.

"Francine, this money belongs to the citizens of Highmore, and I say let's ride there and return it."

"I agree, and maybe we can rent a hotel room there that won't catch on fire and has a lock on the door."

Francine had a mischievous grin on her lovely face. Hugh laughed with good humor. This woman was a perfect match to his expectations. He mounted his horse, keeping a grip on the reins of the riderless horses and they both rode south toward the town of Highmore.

The day became hot and the sun baked them. It was nearly afternoon before some of the buildings of Highmore appeared in the distance. They rode into town and looked for the sheriff's office. They found it easily enough and stopped to dismount. Tying all four horses to the hitchrail, they entered the office.

The sheriff sat at his desk reading a newspaper. He glanced up as the two entered his office. The man was in his later middle life and the gray had crept into his hair and droopy mustache.

"Hello folks, what can I do for you?"

"Sheriff, it's what we can do for you today that is the main thing," Hugh replied.

The man looked puzzled and growled an answer, "The only thing you could do to make me happy would be to help me get a line on those outlaws that robbed our bank."

Hugh managed a knowing grin. *"They were riding a roan with two white forelegs, and a line dun with a white blaze on its nose and someone put a bullet into one of the outlaws."*

The sheriff looked sharply at Hugh. *"What do you know about that robbery?"*

"Well, early this morning we stopped in a grove of trees some miles north of here. Shortly after we arrived, there were two men who galloped up and us, not knowing anything about them, kept quiet. They were speaking of robbing the bank in Highmore and how angry the townspeople were. One of the men was wounded and losing blood. I managed to sneak up on one of them and bend the barrel of my Colt over his hat rack. I had no choice but to shoot the other one dead. We brought their horses along with us and all the money is stuffed in the saddlebags."

The sheriff was stunned and then his eyes brightened. *"Glory be! This turn of events will get me re-elected! Is there anything I can do for you folks? I mean anything."*

"Well, just point us toward a hotel in this town that has a bathtub, locks on the doors, and has never had a fire," Hugh replied.

"I'll do better than that. I'm going to pay for your room and buy you both a dinner."

Hugh glanced at Francine with a smile. Maybe, just maybe, this time they would be able to accomplish what they both hungered for. It was more than lust. His whole body needed to extinguish the frustration of being so close to the moment of joining then being disappointed. He sensed Francine was even more frustrated than he.

They followed the sheriff out the door and to the hitchrack where the four horses stood baking in the sun. The sheriff took the saddlebags off the outlaws' horses and turned back toward his office. Francine looked toward Hugh with doubt in her expression, but Hugh just shrugged and followed the sheriff. He dumped the contents of both bags on his desk. Neither Hugh nor Francine had ever in their lives seen so much money all in one pile.

The sheriff grabbed a large bundle of banded twenty-dollar bills and handed it to Hugh. He handed another bundle to Francine.

"You folks deserve this reward and I hate that miserly banker. Let's us just keep this between us and he will never know about it. Serves the miserable skinflint right!"

Hugh was surprised. There was probably 50 bills in each package and that added up to $1000 each. The sheriff must really be at odds with the banker in that case.

"We thank you, Sheriff, and it shall remain our secret."

No wonder the sheriff had been so generous. He had probably planned this all along. Hugh shoved the bundle of money into his pocket and Francine slipped her money inside her blouse.

"Just go down this street and turn left at the third block. The Imperial Rest is on that quiet side street, and they have a fine restaurant just two doors down from the hotel. I just can't thank you folks enough for what you've done for me and the hard-working people of this town."

He reached out and shook both their hands. Francine's dainty hand was nearly lost in his gnarled fist, but it was a gentle handshake. They left the sheriff's office and went to their horses in the late-afternoon glare of the sun. Little dust devils skipped along the street, darting and staggering like the town drunk with a full load. They mounted their horses and slowly walked them down the street and around the corner. The Imperial Rest was an imposing three-story structure and the street was indeed quiet. They stabled their horses across the street and walked hand in hand, carrying their saddlebags toward the hotel.

The decor of the lobby was just as grand as the impressive outside had been. Brocade draperies covered the windows. A grand chandelier with more than 20 coal oil lamps hung down from the high ceiling. The floors were carpeted with Oriental rugs and the horsehair sofas were invitingly soft looking.

They stepped up to the ornate registry desk. The clerk was clean shaven and he was attired in a white shirt with a tie. This was indeed a high-class hotel.

"Will you sign the register, please?" the pleasant clerk asked, turning the register around to face Hugh. With a glance and a smile at Francine, Hugh scratched "Mr. & Mrs. Hugh Rexler" on the register and handed the clerk a $10 gold piece.

"Boy, front!" the clerk spoke sharply. *"Please lead these guests to room 22 rear and take their saddlebags. Here, sir, is the key to room 22."*

They followed the bellhop up the carpeted stairs and a short way down the hall to their room. They stopped in front of their room and Hugh handed the man his key. As the door opened, both were amazed at the grandeur of their room. A four-poster bed with a canopy of fringed roping stood solidly at one end of the room. The floor was carpeted and the walls papered with a pleasing pattern of flowers. There was a nightstand on either side of the bed, each with its own lamp. Two overstuffed chairs lounged against the opposite walls. There was a writing desk off to the right with a wooden chair pushed up to it.

"*Sir?*" the bellboy said.

Hugh turned to face him. The man probably wanted a tip.

"*Sir and madam, the bath is just down at the end of the hall, and when you are ready, just pull the bellcord near the head of the bed and someone will fill the tub for you.*"

Hugh reached into his pocket and then dropped a half-dollar in the bellboy's hand.

"*Thank you, sir.*" The bellboy bowed and left through the door, closing it quietly behind him.

"*Hugh, this is the most elegant room I have ever been in. I want to take a bath, of course, but first I want to shop for some clothes. I'm sure you can understand how much I need to get out of these trail-worn clothes.*"

"*We have more or less struck it lucky, I'd say, and I agree let's both buy some new clothes. We can sure afford it now, thanks to the generous sheriff of this town. I wonder how much the sheriff will keep for himself?*"

Francine laughed gaily. "*I'm certain he will be just as generous with his own share too. Who can blame him? Thirty dollars a month isn't too much to thrive on, but with an added bonus he will be able to live comfortably. I wonder, Hugh, will he give any of it back to the banker?*"

"That's something I hadn't even thought about, but I'm sure he will have mercy on the townspeople and give back the larger share of it."

After the locking the door behind themselves, they descended the stairs and stopped by the desk to ask the clerk where the dry goods store was located. He told them there was one just a half-block down the street on the opposite side.

Chapter 3

Hugh and Francine entered the dry goods store together. He picked out a plain red flannel shirt and another that was blue checkered, a pair of jeans, two pairs of socks, and a pair of longjohns. Francine wandered through the dresses, skirts, blouses, underclothes, and nightwear. She found a dress she liked, and she picked out some undergarments, a new skirt and blouse, and a very appealing and revealing nightgown with a lacy hem. Finally, she got some jeans and a flannel shirt.

She had never in her young life had the funds to pick and choose what she wanted, and this was like a trip to the penny-candy store with a whole dollar to spend. Francine was smiling broadly as she toted her choices to the counter. She glanced around the store and Hugh was nowhere in sight. He must have made his purchases and gone back to the hotel. The clerk added up her purchases and told her she owed a whole $6.35. Francine turned her back to the clerk and reached into her blouse. She pulled one of the $20 bills from the banded pack and then turned around to hand it to the clerk. He counted out $13.65 from a cigar box he kept under the counter and handed it to her. He wrapped her purchases in brown paper and thanked her as she left the store.

There she saw Hugh come out of the general store three doors down the street. There was an odd look on his face, somewhat happy but tinged with guilt. What on earth had he bought in there? Naturally she was puzzled and being a woman, she would find a way to discover what it was. Hugh spied Francine as she exited the dry goods store. His effort to conceal his expression was not successful and he knew Francine would be on his case to find out what he'd bought in the general store.

"Francine, before you even ask, I bought something for you in there and I want it to be a surprise, so let's just mosey back to the hotel."

Francine loved surprises and could hardly wait to see what it was. They entered the hotel lobby and the bellboy rushed over to offer to carry their purchases up the stairs.

"No thank you, but would you please have the bathtub

filled?" Hugh tossed the bellboy a quarter. With a big smile, the bellboy rushed up the stairs two at a time. Hugh and Francine followed at a slower pace. Hugh unlocked their door and opened it for her to precede him into the room. She placed her package on the bed and watched Hugh put his clothes on a chair.

"Hugh, what's your surprise?" She was anxious to know.

Without a word, he stepped in front of her and fell to his knees. He took her hand in his and kissed it.

"Francine, will you do the honor of becoming my wife?"

He reached into his pocket and withdrew a diamond ring. Francine was stunned and nearly speechless. A big surprise it was! She knew in her heart she wanted to be with Hugh, but she had no idea he was so serious about her. Did she want to spend the rest of her life with Hugh? There was no question in her mind. She fell to her knees in front of him and wrapped her arms around him. As she kissed him again and again, she managed so speak.

"Oh, yes yes yes Hugh. I will!"

Hugh stood and helped her to her feet, wrapping her in his arms and kissing her deeply and passionately.

"That's the answer I was hoping for, darling."

As the daylight began to fade, there was a rap on the door. The bellboy stood there announcing that the bath was ready.

"You're about two hours early," Hugh replied.

"Sir?" the bellboy was confused.

"Nevermind, it's a joke, here's another quarter."

The bellboy left with a happy grin on his homely face.

"Francine, the bath is yours," he invited. As she left the

room carrying her package, Hugh thought about a candlelight supper for the two of them. He sat on one of the chairs and planned it all out. Soon enough, the door opened and a dream appeared. Francine was clad in a frilly nightgown, her damp hair slicked back. She was glowing with happiness. Here was the real thing. Francine.

He quickly picked up his package and went to the bathroom at the end of the hall. He stripped quickly and slid into the warm water. He only soaked a few minutes and then quickly bathed, rinsed off, dried with a fluffy towel, and dressed in his new clothes. As he entered their room, Francine was standing by the four-poster bed. She looked beautiful, provocative, and serious.

"Hugh, come here and undress me." she demanded.

Hugh was tempted to play the part of a raging animal, but with quivering hands he carefully removed her gown, exploring each new part of her body. The silence was broken only by the heavy breathing of each partner. When he enfolded her in his embrace, he felt the now-familiar mild electric shock of skin meeting skin. It was a sensuous and pleasurable luxury as they lay holding each other. Francine fiercely kissed him and tightened her arms around him, slowly sliding her body under him.

"Francine, don't you think it would be better to wait until we speak our vows?" He joked.

"HUSH UP, Hugh, and love me!"

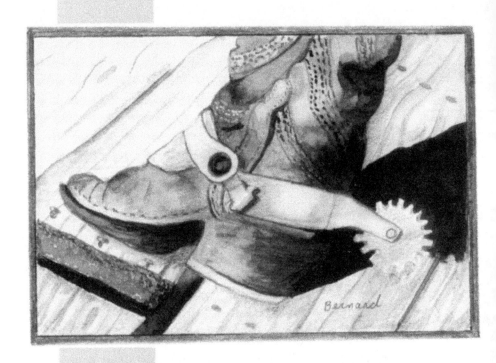

LINCOLN'S
LAW

WAITING ON THE WANTED

Chapter 1

Linc sat in his office, heels up on the battered desk. The afternoon was hot and dry, as he thumbed thru the wanted posters. Some of the older ones were dog-eared, and creased nearly to a point of being useless. The summer sun streamed thru the fly specked windowpane, and illuminated one corner of the room. Dust motes floated in their orbits disturbed only by the occasional breeze that wafted thru the open door. Two mentally retarded flies bumped their heads against the glass, in an inane contest to see which would fall unconscious first.

The nondescript tabby cat watched this action with tail twitching, seemingly not able to raise enough interest to bat the silly insects into oblivion. *'She must be pregnant again'* Linc surmised. She always got lazy when she was full of kittens and motherhood, it appeared, was her natural state. He couldn't remember how many litters of kittens she'd produced in her short life, and not two, it seemed, had looked identical. Sort of reminded Linc of his first wife. She had the same attitude and outlook on life as this common alley cat. She'd broken his heart during their first year of marriage and Linc had never begun a meaningful relationship with any woman again.

He reached into his vest pocket, and extracted a thin cheroot. Biting off the end, he scratched a match on the scarred desktop. The rich blue smoke mixed, and rose with the dancing dustmotes ceilingward.

"Deputy?"

The squeaky, high pitched voiced banker broke the afternoon silence. He hadn't heard the sneaky little pipsqueak come in, and it startled him. No doubt he was here to complain about the town drunk urinating on his gold lettered plate glass entrance door again. Why, oh why didn't that lush get run down by a freight wagon, or maybe the afternoon stage, and do everybody a big favor? *"Because, I guess, the Good Lord watches over drunks, and idiots"* Linc smiled to himself.

"What kin I do fer yuh, Rawlind?" Linc put the reward posters on his desk, and took the stogie out of his mouth.

"Deputy, I'm concerned about the unkempt, down and out looking character, who has been lounging in my bank. He's watching the money my customers have been depositing this afternoon." The banker sniffed.

Linc mentally laughed off the banker's worries, as most cowboys looked down, and out. What did he expect when even the best of the lot, made all of forty dollars a month, and usually let it slip thru their workworn fingers with wine, women, and song, as the saying goes, when payday rolled around.

"He bin botherin' yer customers, er yer employees?" Linc asked the man, wishing the cat would bat Rawlind into oblivion.

"Well......er no not actually, but anyone can see he's been casing my bank, and I'm certain he has one, or more partners just waiting about for the word." Rawlind explained nervously wringing his dry hands. *"Are you going to do something?"* the banker insisted.

"Yup, I'll have uh talk with the gent, an' set yer mind at ease."

Lincoln sighed, knowing full well the banker wasn't going to cut him any slack, until he did. It had felt good resting his bum leg on the desktop, but he just knew it couldn't last. He swung his legs off the desk, and pushed the wanted posters into the right hand drawer. He retrieved his Stetson from the desktop, and adjusted it to his liking, brim down to shade his grey eyes. The banker scurried his mousey way back to the money house, but Linc wasn't going to be in a big rush to follow.

Really this should be a job for the town marshal, but of course there was none. The last fellow had quit in disgust, and no one could blame him for it, as the town council had decided they couldn't afford to pay him the thirty dollars set aside every month for his wages. The sheriff usually kept pretty much to his office in Wellington, the seat of Sumner County, Kansas, about ten miles east. So that left Linc nearly all of the Western half to take care of. Not that he couldn't cover it, but it grated on his sense of fairness, and he wished the town council wasn't such a group of cheapskates. He limped the first few steps toward the doorway, but as he crossed the threshold, the pain seemed to magically melt away. *'To hell with the banker. A stop at the Cartwheel for a cool foamy beer. That's the ticket'* Linc decided.

He peered over the batwings, to check the action. There wasn't much going on. A three handed poker game at one of the deal tables, and a couple of ranch owners, Cap Morrison, and Hack Dorfer were sipping on one of the better brands of whiskey. The bottle was on the bartop in front of them. The piano player was tuning the upright piano with the aid of a pitch pipe, and doing a fair job of it. The saloon instrument couldn't keep it's tones pure for more than a day or two at the most and needed frequent attention.

Linc entered the saloon, and bellied up to the bar, resting his bum leg on the brass rail.

"Beer." he told the bartender, Fellows, who looked as though he'd missed his calling as an undertaker. Tall, and lean with a long mournful face. His Adam's apple was as prominent a feature as the ears that stood out from his head, like two open gates. The drooping

dark brown mustache completed the undertaker image. Fellows drew a cool one and placed it in front of Linc.

"Lazy afternoon, Linc, but that tinhorn cardshark has been double dealin' off the bottom of the deck, an' neither of them cowboys has caught him at it as yet, but I feel it comin', an' it's only a matter of time until one or both ventilate his personality with a couple of lead reminders." Fellows spoke low enough so only the deputy could hear.

Linc watched the card play in the bar back mirror. Fellows was right and the tinhorn was getting sloppy with over confidence. His first swallow of beer was always the best, wetting the whistle on the way down. He put the mug back on the bar.

"Bartender, more whiskey over here," one of the cowboys ordered. Fellows came out from behind the bar with a half full bottle of bar whiskey and headed for the trio. The piano player had finished with his tuning, and was earnestly playing "Buffalo Gal" on the ivory keys, his derby hat cocked at a juanty angle. The bartender filled glasses all round and returned to his station at the bar end. Linc finished his beer in one long gulp, and left a nickel on the bar for payment.

"Gotta roust a bozo outa the bank. He's got Mister 'pass the cheese' Rawland peeing all over himself with worry ...spose he's afraid he's gonna git stuck up fer alla his cash money." He grinned at Fellows, as he left. The bartender smiled back. He wasn't a big fan of the money lender either.

At that instant, the stage rolled into the depot trailing a long plume of dust. The driver sawed the reins, and stomped on the brake to bring the rig to a stop. The shotgun guard was slumped over in his seat.

"Whoa!, yuh ornery critters. Hey, wake up Barnes, we're heah."

The guard stirred himself, and streched with a big yawn rubbing his eyes. Linc wondered how the man could sleep thru the rough and tumble ride, but then some folks could sleep on a bucking bronco it seemed. The horses appeared happy to come to a halt. They were glistening with sweat and lathered. The stage driver climbed down to catch the baggage, as the guard tossed it off the top of the stage.

Passengers climbed down, as Linc watched. There were four today. A salesman with a dusty sample case, a range rider, whose saddle had been tossed off the stage top into the dust, a young fellow who appeared to be a surveyor, or possibly a mining engineer and an elderly grey haired lady dressed in a black high neck dress. The younger man helped her down from the stage coach.

Linc had spent much of his life sizing up people and a law officer must sometimes stake his life on this judgement. There was something about the elderly lady that didn't quite ring true. Nothing he could put his finger on, but a subtle difference most people would never notice. She carried a reticule with black drawstrings that appeared to be somewhat heavier than average. Her grey tresses were neatly coiffeured in short curls, under a tight fitting bonnet. It was the hair. It seemed to Linc the hairdo was nearly perfect, and he wondered how that was possible after riding the stagecoach all day. He spotted a gold wedding band on her left hand that had been worn thin by the passing years. Her face was careworn, and discourged looking.

Linc dismissed the uncertainty for the moment and walked to the Mayfield Bank and Trust. He entered the doorway and was puzzled, as everything seemed normal, with the teller waiting on customers, and putting money away. As he scanned the bank, he failed to see any scruffy looking character Rawlind had described lounging about and was inclined to believe the banker was paranoid on the subject of bad guys.

Linc turned to leave and the gent in question appeared at the entrance doorway. The mans face regestered shock as he noticed the deputy striding in his direction.

"Mister, yuh had better have a good reason fer hangin' 'bout in here."

Linc spoke quietly, but firmly as he stepped in front of the man, who appeared to be memorizing Linc's face. He mentally reviewed the reward posters he'd been studying a short time ago. This rider didn't seem to resemble any of the ones with faces drawn on them and none of the physical descriptions matched. The man was short and thin. About five foot five, a hundred thirty-five in weight, with a gray and black peppered full moustache. He was carrying a short barreled Colt .45 in an open, worn holster. The squinted, muddy brown eyes, that had maybe seen too much violence. His thin, flared nose had been broken at least once.

"Deputy." the man answered, "is there someplace we can talk?"

"Right here is fine an' dandy." Linc replied cooly.

"No, sir, I'm a Federal Marshal, and what I have to tell you isn't for public knowledge." The man explained.

Two shots, that were so close together they almost seemed as one, exploded the afternoon tranquility. A short pause, and then another shot.

"My office, later Marshal." Lincoln retorted tersely, and headed out the door.

It almost had to be the Cartwheel and his suspicions were confirmed as that was the direction, it appeared, everyone was headed. Linc shouldered his way inside. The scene was only too familiar. The tinhorn lay still on the floor, one leg folded under, in a widening pool of blood. His chair lay on it's side near the table. Close to his left hand was a .41 caliber two shot Derringer hideout gun pointed toward the far wall. One of the cowboys still sat in his chair, bleeding from a serious wound high, and to the right of the center of his chest. His face pale, and drawn as the shock began to wear off.

Linc knelt by the gambler, who's sightless eyes stared ceilingward. He was dead, if the position of the two bullet wounds in his chest were any indication. They were high, and low, but close together, and it appeared either of the shots should have been fatal. Cards were scattered on the floor, and upon the deal table, along with a few double eagles. The other cowboy, who'd been in the game, stood close by with a look of concern on his rugged face.

"Stop me iffin I'm wrong" Lincoln began, *"yuh caught the tinhorn double dealin', an' called 'im on it, then as he drew his hideout, one of yuh busted 'is brisket with a couple uh lead stoppers."*

"Matter 'o fact we both plugged 'im Deputy. Tommy here, drawed an' fired at the same time the tinhorn did. Even after Tommy's bullet hit 'im, thet slicker turned his gun in mah direction, so I let 'im have it, too."

"I tole yuh, Linc, there was gonna be trouble. Yuh shoulda run thet double dealin' pasteboard flipper on up the road." Fellows complained, *"now I gotta mess tuh scrub offin the floor. Yuh know how blood begins tuh stink in this here heat."*

"Somebody git the sawbones 'fore Tommy leaks alla his blood out," The uninjured cowpoke pleaded. Apparently someone already had, as Doc Hutchison pushed through the crowded doorway.

"Believe the tinhorn's beyond help, Doc, but see iffin yuh kin patch up Tommy, here." Linc urged, knowing how fiesty Doc was about someone telling him how to practice medicine, but on the other hand it might save some time the wounded cowboy needed.

Doc knelt near the fallen gambler and held a small mirror near the man's mouth, and nose. Shaking his head, he rose to attend the living.

"Some of you gents help carry this man up tuh my office across the street. Thet bullet has gotta come out." Doc ordered.

The request was obeyed quickly, as every man on the spot was thinking: *'There, but for the grace of God, sit I,'* as a stray bullet could have anyones name on it, and didn't play favorites. Four of them carried Tommy out the door. Linc left the saloon to return to his office. He arrived to find the Marshal sitting by his desk, and smoking a large cigar. The whole room reeked of burning rope, and hot tar.

"Whot duh yuh call them seegars?" Linc asked, rubbing his smarting eyes.

"They's called 'Painted Ladies' an' I buys em ten fer a nickel." the man explained. *"I'm Hiram Burns, Federal Marshal, workin' outa Wichita."* The man showed his badge, and continued, *"We've reason tuh believe the bank, here in town, will be held up in the very near future. I'm gonna assume thet tomorrah bein' Friday, an' also the last day o' the month, there will be a sizeable amount of cash on hand. I doubt iffin yuh've received a reward dodger on Edgar Choates, alias 'Molly Malone'?"*

Hiram paused, and seemed to be waiting for conformation.

"No, sir I ain't," Linc answered.

"This here bank buster dresses up like a little ole gray haired lady, an' I swear yud never tumble tuh fact it was really a man." This statement stirred a memory in Linc's line of thought, but he couldn't quite bring it into focus. The Marshal droned on about the jobs this outlaw had pulled, and gotten clean away from. As everybody had spent their time looking for somebody's maiden aunt, who didn't exist for more than a few moments during the bank holdup. In reality he'd packed the granny clothes, and rode off like a real cowpoke. The lady off the stage! That was it, Linc knew there was something about the way she carried herself, and the too perfect hairdo had to be a wig.

"Ah believe, Marshal, thet gent climbed offin the stage uh short time ago, dressed, an' made up like yuh've described, as uh little ole lady. Somethin' 'bout the way she carried herself, din't strike me as natural. So how yuh spose we go 'bout corralin' this joker?" Linc wanted to know.

"Yuh leave thet tuh me, as no one here 'bout, but you and Rawlind, will know who Ah' am. Ah'm gonna stake out the bank lobby, an' either give 'im ah chance tuh surrender, er gun the sucker down. One way er t'other Ah plan tuh end his career." Burns related.

"Ah'll tell yuh one bit uh news, Marshal, yuh scared the poop outa ar town banker, he thinks yer ah casin' his bank."

Linc smiled at the thought.

"Ah spose Ah better clue the gent in for he fills his trousers, but kin he be relied on tuh keep 'is yap shut?" Burns questioned.

"Iffin he believes yer gonna save his bank, he'll probably wag his tail, an' lick yer hand." Linc laughed, and rose to shake the Marshal's hand.

As the man left his office, Linc sunk once again into his chair. If Mr. U.S. Marshal was gonna take care of the bank job hisself, that was fine and dandy. Lincoln knew his own limitations. He wasn't a fast draw, but had always made his first shot hit the mark he was aiming at. He'd worked at the fast draw hour after hour, but some persons were never meant to be gunslicks. Anyhow he had better things to do than wet nurse a spooky banker.

RAWLIND'S PAST

Chapter 2

Rawlind sat comfortably in his chair behind his massive oaken desk he'd paid a premium to have hauled from St. Louis. It was one of the few consessions he'd allowed himself. Not that he was a spendthrift, but why not flaunt it if you've got it, was his motto. The deputy had spoken briefly to the stranger who'd been lounging about the lobby, and the fellow had left shortly after Linc had gone to investigate the shooting at the Cartwheel. He'd not returned and maybe he was done with him.

He removed one of the fine Cuban cigars from the humidor on his desk and snipped the end off with the silver plated clip that had been a gift from Edith. Rolling the cigar around in his mouth, while he searched his brocaded vest pocket for a match, gave him a pleasant taste and aroma of the excellent tobacco. He scratched the match under the arm of his chair and fired the end of his smoke, until it was evenly lit. Leaning back in his chair, with arms folded across his chest, eyes closed, body relaxed and legs crossed he daydreamed about his past life and the living standard he enjoyed at the present time. The fine house built on a slight rise, east of Mayfield, was just enough higher than the rest of the houses. He could look down on the rest of the population and it made him feel like a prince in a land of paupers.

His early life had been hard work in the fact that he'd used any means at hand to get ahead. Frequently stepping on the toes of friendship and trust. Lie, cheat, steal and murder? Everything but murder, unless you counted Edith, and you really couldn't count her as she had greeted her maker with a soft smile on her homley face.

Rawlind had worked for her father and skimmed the take in a manner the old duffer had never discovered. Then he'd married Edith. Lonely, homely, rich Edith. He romanced the neglected spinster with promises, flowers, suave urbane manners and sold her the phony, hollow shell that wasn't really him. After the honeymoon was over and he had gained control of her substantial fortune, he quietly drove her insane by means he'd rather not think about. They still haunted his worst nightmares, but never bothered his conscience at all.

This wealth had given him his start and by careful invest-
ment, only the safest of loans, along with paying out the tiniest per-
centage of interest on savings, he'd managed to amass enough so he
could live a life of ease and sweep his soiled past into the closet. It
had been a rush when he'd told the deputy "NO" when the man had
applied for a loan. He had justified it by explaining what a poor risk
any lawman was. Why he could be gunned down at any moment and
then who would repay the loan?

Linc had seemed angry at the time, but hadn't drawn his
money out of savings. Actually the man had managed to put away
around two hundred forty dollars a year and in the eleven years he'd
been deputy sheriff he had saved nearly twenty seven hundred dollars. He'd wanted the loan, as he had revealed, to buy up some land
he liked the looks of. Rawlind figured he'd actually done the man a
favor, as the land had been overpriced and the proof was evident.
That land was still for sale.

His thoughts were interrupted by a voice he didn't recognize:

"Mister Rawlind?"

He opened his eyes and nearly died of fright. It was the
scruffy appearing cowpoke who had been hanging around his lobby
all day. His heart was racing like a triphammer and he began to gasp.

*"Sorry sir, Ah didn't mean tuh startle yuh. Ah'm Burns, fed-
eral marshal Burns, an' Ah have some information you'd have some
interest in."* The man paused. Rawlind began to relax, but his heart
still pounded with excitement.

*"We've reason tuh believe there's uh gent in town, who plans
to rob your bank on Friday afternoon when he has reason tuh believe yud have plenty of cash on hand. Now Ah'm gonna be in the
lobby, 'cause this geezer don't know me. He'll be made up to look
like uh elderly woman, an' has used this disguise successfully. Ah
aim tuh end his career one way er other, so iffen yuh kin keep ut
under yer hat so tuh speak, Ah'm shore this matter kin be taken care
of with nobody gittin hurt, er yer bank losin' money."*

Rawlind took in all the marshal had told him. It had sounded good, but in his experience, it seemed, there was a wide margin for error.

He planed to have the teller keep minimum amount of cash in the cage at all times until this problem was resolved. He glanced at the grandfather clock by the wall and realized it was past closing time.

"Marshal Burns, you do what you have to, but I'm going to make plans of my own, which include having the teller keep a minimum amount of cash in the teller's cage. I won't tell him why I want him to empty his cash drawer every fifteen minutes, but I am sure the man will figure it out for himself. I sincerely hope this won't tip off your bank robber. If it does though, I'm sorry, but my first consideration must be to the banks investors." Rawlind explained.

"This yahoo has plenty of experience, an' A'm afeared it just might give him a clue. So a different plan on mah part will have to be formulated." The lawman seemed somewhat put out by Rawlind's revelation.

Rawlind didn't speak aloud, but his thoughts were: *"Well, too bad, but its my bank and my money at stake. All you have to worry about is chasing and catching thevies, so good luck Mr Federal Marshal!"*

The marshal left the bank in deep thought and the money lender was busy for the next hour balancing ledgers, stowing the cash in the vault and locking up the bank for the night. As he left by the front door he cursed to himself as he glanced at the stain on the gold lettering on the door. If he EVER caught the town drunk urinating on his front door, there weren't going to be any more complaints to the deputy. No sir! Complaints hadn't solved the problem, so he would handle it in his own way. He had caused people to disappear permanently. Not in this town, of course, but he had discovered a method, matter of fact a perfect solution to this type of problem. Just let him catch that dreg of humanity with his doohickey in hand and it would be good night to that lush forever! And it didn't cost much to get the job done either.

Rawlind turned the key in the lock of the front door and walked the short distance to the livery stable. Here he kept his spring buggy with curtains on the sides to keep the weather out and his matched set of bay horses. The liveryman already had his team hitched up. They were prancing and pawing the turf.

"Evenin' Mr. Rawlind, got yer team in harness, rarin' tuh go."

The hostler smiled, with cap in hand. Rawlind blessed the man with a smile. That's all he really needed as he paid him what he believed to be a more than adequate sum to take care of his team and buggy. So far he had been satisfied with the results. Maybe, just maybe he would surprise the man with a small gift at Christmas time, but that all would depend on how he acted until that time.

Rawlind stepped up into his buggy and slapped his team smartly with the reins. They trotted off with a pace he enjoyed and could show off how well his team was matched. As they trotted up the street, he waved and smiled at the people who owed him money. They, of course, had no choice in the matter of returning his greeting. No matter how much many of them probably hated him.

Foreclosure was a fact of life and Rawlind took great delight in riding out with the deputy sheriff to move the unlucky off their properties. These people knew that one late payment would bring down the wrath of Rawlind and a very good chance of losing their happy homes. Only Rawlind and the Good Lord knew just how much property he had squirreled away in the twelve years he had owned the bank.

The last owner, who had given the citizens of this community too much credit and waited too long to collect his accounts, and had felt too much kindness for his fellow man, was forced to close his bank and sell to Rawlind for twenty percent of it's true value. That's the shrewd manner in which he conducted his banking business. That was the reason he was so successful, although he could count his friends on one hand and have four fingers left over.

He smiled to himself as he turned up the long lane leading to his magnificent home surrounded by mighty oak trees. Nothing made him happier than the sight of all he had accomplished.

Choates' Chance

Chapter 3

Choates, in his Molly Malone guise, had taken a room at Mayfield's only hotel. In the afternoon heat it was a relief to shed his disguise and lie on the bed to relax. He didn't envy women their corsets, bustles and high necked dresses with long sleeves in this unsufferable weather. It was no wonder some fainted when the temperature rose. This was definatly a one-horse town and he couldn't wait for dark to see if they would roll up the boardwalks when the sun went down.

How, he wondered, did they live out their lives just watching the grass grow, or lining up to watch the barber cut hair? he figured the big event of the day would be watching a spotted dog cross the street without getting run over by the twice a day stage coach. Why surely there was big money, nickels and dimes even, bet on the mutts athletic ability. How do they keep from going quietly insane? He wondered. Give him the bright lights and hustle of St Louis, Dodge City, or San Francisco. Now those were places where a man could find whatever it took to scratch an itch. Oh well, it must take a certain type of mentality to be able to tolerate BORING.

He suspected the Federal Marshal Burns, who had stumbled onto his ploy shortly after his last 'break the bank' caper in Dodge City, had or soon would arrive in town. He knew without a doubt the man had been on his trail ever since then and would be like a bulldog with a bone and never let go.

Busting this bank might seem to some an unsurmountable task, but to him it was a way of life. A quick study of human nature gave him all the edge he had ever needed. Part of the thrill was matching wits with the lawdogs. He knew Burns was a lone wolf and a proud, vain man.

In fact he could nearly read the marshal's mind. Surely he would have a talk with that sleepy-eyed deputy he had spotted, watching the passengers down off the stage. The deputy was slow moving with his gimpy leg and appeared to have a slow witted manner, but underestimating opponents was a fatal way of ending a promising career and that was the last thing he wanted to do! Besides making a good living, he was having fun.

He decided, even with the knowledge Burns would share with the local county mountie, the man would insist on working alone... wanting to take all the credit for ending the string of holdups. Choates believed, as he was holding up the teller, Burns would call on him to give himself up, gun still in its holster, believing himself to be the fastest gunslick federal marshal west of the Red River Valley. That in itself would give him all the edge he needed to whirl and shoot that proud man through the heart. *"We'll see,"* he smiled to himself, *"whose career comes to an end."*

Unknown to most, he had a partner to hold his getaway horse and take care of the granny clothes after the robbery. This man was very dependable and had always been paid part of the take. The man had no discernable imagination and seemed very happy not to take part in the actual holdup. Loyalty, it seemed, could be purchased with ease if one picked the right turkey.

Choates turned over on his side and sat up on the edge of the bed. Taking papers and a sack of Bull Durham off the washstand, he expertly rolled himself a smoke and fired it up. The tobacco would satisfy his nicotine urge, but his thirst was another vulture sitting on the dead limb of habit. He'd seen a saloon down in the middle of the next block called the Cartwheel, if memory served, and a good memory was one of the best companions to ride the trail with. Every jerkwater, whistle stop town, it seemed, had either a Cartwheel, Silver Dollar, or a Golden Nugget saloon gracing one of its main drags. No originality in choosing a name, just go with the flow.

He finished his cigarette and dropped the smoldering butt into the wash basin. He poured a few drops of water from the pitcher to make sure the embers were out before he turned to open the oversize handbag containing a worn pair of jeans and a cotton plaid shirt. He shook them to smooth out the wrinkles and put the clothes on. The low boots he kept in the bottom of the bag, needed a shine, but that could wait. Of course he would have to find a hat as that was one item that couldn't be hidden in handbag. It had always been easy to steal one from a peg in a hashhouse as men were of the habit of paying most attention to what they were putting into their mouths and watching their headgear was unimportant at that time.

Choates partly opened the door and peered up and down the hallway. Nobody was about. He stepped out and headed for the stairs. The room clerk didn't look up from the newspaper he was engrossed in. The late afternoon sun baked the dusty town with its brassy illumination. Little dust devils skipped down the street on twirling toes, to dissipate into nothingness like ghosts that had never been.

There was a crowd dispersing from in front of the saloon when he arrived and without any urging, one of the gawkers told him a couple of cowboys had ventilated a clumbsy card flipper, who they had caught double dealing off the bottom of the deck, with a couple of Colonel Colt's lead projectiles.

He wondered, without much hope, if they had anything decent on the barback to drink. The regular rotgut served in these places always turned his stomach to a churning mass of cramps and he was convinced they sprinkled ground glass into it just to cause him pain. He pushed aside the batwing doors and caught the tinkle of a slightly out of tune piano the key pounder was thumping on.

The bartender was sprinkling new sawdust on the floor to cover a damp spot. His mop and bucket stood near the far end of the bar. Choates studied the bottles on the bar back but didn't see any of the premium brands he was used to. That was another minus for this jerkwater town. The bartender had finished with his chores and returned the mop and bucket to the back room.

"Whiskey, mister?" Fellows eyed the stranger. It wasn't anyone he'd ever seen before. It had to be someone off the afternoon stage. One glance at the soft hands told him this dude didn't do any rough work for a living and he placed him in a surveyor or mining engineer category.

"Do you have anything under the bar besides that sandbur and ground glass firewater?" Choates wanted to know.

Fellows eyed him with new respect. This gent evidently had more that a few coins to jingle and was asking for some of the good stuff in the dusty bottles that most of the cowboys here and about couldn't or wouldn't lay down their dimes for.

"Yes indeed, how does Bower's Blend, or Hammond's Straight Kentucky, take hold of yuh Sir?"

Fellows was surprised that any saloon this far from the city lights would stock any of the good brands. *"Hammond's is my favorite, so bring it on."*

The barkeep reached far under the counter and brought forth a nearly fill bottle of Hammond's and wiped off the dust with his bar rag. *"As yuh can see, Ah don't sell the good stuff often. The range rannies in these parts hate to part with their coins. Matter uh fact most uh them squeeze their nickels 'til them bufferlos beller fer mercy."* Fellows grinned at his own wit. *"Yuh jist passin' thru, mister?"*

Choates sipped the whiskey slowly. Damn! but this whiskey was smooth. Maybe he should buy the whole bottle and take it back to his hotel room...No, he couldn't. There was a job to do tomorrow that wouldn't tolerate a hangover and his very life depended on it. Better just enjoy a couple of drinks and then retire to be bright eyed and bushy tailed the next day.

"Just passin' through and you can fill this again when I get it empty, but no more than two drinks. Maybe I'll come back Friday and buy whats left in the bottle." Choates mentioned.

He finished the last sip and held his glass out for a refill. He watched as a cowboy swept one of the barmaids into his arms and began to dance around the room in time with the piano plunkers rythum. Dance wasn't really the proper description. Obviously the cowpoke was carrying a full load of firewater and was only keeping his balance with the aid of the hefty barmaid. The strain of the heavy load was beginning to tell on the poor lady and she was desperatly trying to think her way out of this situation. It was solved for her as the cowboy stumbled and fell to the floor, out cold.

"How much for the drinks?" He asked.

"Twenty cents total, my friend."

Choats didn't reply to that. Friends he could do without in his line of work. He dug into his pocket and dropped a quarter on the bartop. Fellows scooped up the coin and dropped a nickel in its place.

He then moved down the bar to re-fill an empty glass. Choates finished his second drink. That was going to have to be it for this session. He had a Friday appointment with a bag full of greenbacks. He picked up his change and stepped away from the bar. Waiting by the batwings, as three dusty range riders stepped through, giving him a quick glance.

The street was the same except for the fact the sun had slipped a bit lower on its trip to the horizion. Low enough so he wished for a hat to shade his eyes.

He left the saloon and as he crossed a side street, on his way back to the hotel, he met the sleepy eyed deputy. The lawman's expression didn't change and he appeared to have something on his mind. It wasn't recognition as the last time they'd met, he'd been in his Molly Malone disguise. It was a game. Fooling the people, especially the lawdogs. Choates entered the hotel lobby and sat on an easychair until nearly suppertime going over his plans and drawing the layout of the bank on a scrap of paper.

Shortly after the day clerk had been replaced by his night counterpart, Choates stepped up to the desk and asked the clerk, *"Where's the best place to get a good meal in this town?"*

The clerk was busy counting money and checking all the pidgeon holes for mail.

Without looking around he replied, *"Tonight is beef stew night at Flo's Boardinghouse. It's a block over and right in the middle of the block. I know it sounds common, but you'll be missin' the best stew of your life if you pass it up."*

The clerk was enthaustic as he turned to face him. Well, he'd give it a try as there weren't that many choices in this one pony town. It was nearly six by the clock on the lobby wall. He turned and walked out the door.

Linc had been mulling over what the marshal had told him and as he crossed the street he looked up just in time to meet a man coming the other way. The manner in which the man minced his steps and the shape of his face...yep the height was about right. It led him to believe this was the dude he'd seen being helped off the stage. Yep, Molly Malone himself! As their paths met and they both walked on, Lincoln turned back for another look. He was convinced this was the man. He filed this information away and planned to get involved in Friday's holdup no matter what the marshal's wishes were.

Choates found the boarding house with no trouble. It was typical of the eras buildings. Let mother nature take care of it. False front, two story, weathered gray clapboard siding and appeared as though there were at least a dozen rooms which were mostly on the second floor. He entered and discovered a line had already formed. Men and a few women from all walks of life, it would seem. Just gazing along the waiting line he saw cowboys, miners, what appeared to be crewmen from the railroad, well dressed business men, doctor, lawyer, merchant, thief, workman, soldier, but no Indian chief.

Along with most of the men in line, were a few women. Most probably wives, except for the hefty barmaid from the Cartwheel saloon who was probably a painted lady forced to sell her favors to keep the wolf away from her door. This was merely speculation on his part and was part of his usual guessing game. Not his kind of woman in any sense of the word. He was partial to the sweet, young, innocent, shrinking violet type of girl just entering the mysterious age of young womanhood.

Glancing along the wall he spotted at least four hats that would probably fit him and he would, without a doubt, steal one as he left. The aroma of the stew, that was cooking, teased his sense of smell and if it was indeed as good as the aroma, then maybe the hotel clerk knew what he was talking about. Finally the line shuffled forward until he was able to reach the serving table and scooped a generous portion of the stew into his bowl. There were baking powder biscuits, soda crackers, canned fruit, boiled potatoes, strong coffee and glasses of drinking water. A dozen pies were lined up for dessert.

Choates found a place alongside one of the better dressed men and as he sat on a straight banjo back chair, he placed his food on the table, then noticed the brown haired woman who seemed to be in charge of the whole operation. After his first taste of the stew, he realized the night clerk at the hotel knew his beef stew and had to admit to himself this was the best he'd ever had the pleasure of tasting.

Flo, the good looking one in charge, had found a way to put it all together in a class by itself. The cherry pie couldn't be faulted either as he finished his stew and cut into the pie wedge with his fork. The crust was flakey, but firm and the cherries were just tart enough and not overwhelmed with sugar.

He wondered if this Flo was married or spoken for. The meal was nearly enough to make his reconsider his life of crime. Shortly thereafter his question was answered by a brawny giant of a man sitting across the table from him. He refered to her as 'Miss Florence' and the scowl on his face had softened as he spoke of her. His large hands showed the callous of hard labor and if he had eyes for the lady, then Choates decided there wouldn't be any arguement from him.

FLO'S BOARDING HOUSE
Chapter 4

Florence had not yet married and was considered an old maid. To her, twenty-nine was just the right age to be at this time in her life. She had inherited the boarding house from her mother, who at the age of thirty-eight, left town to try her luck in Dodge City, where fortunes were made and lost with amazing regularity. Florence hadn't heard from her in more than a year and feared she had met with an untimely demise. Her only concern, at the present time, was the boarding house. She depended on it for her livelihood.

There were nine steady boarders which she fed three times a day and the large dining hall which could feed fifty patrons at a sitting. It was filled to near capicity each mealtime when it was open to all who came. To the citizens, who had discovered what an excellent chef and organizer she was, there was no place they would rather be when the doors opened. As the mealtime business had grown, especially at the supper hour, she found she could no longer handle it alone. She had hired two people to help out around the kitchen, the dining hall and elsewhere in the boardinghouse.

She found she couldn't handle all the chores with only twenty-fours in the day. This couple she had hired were man and wife, who were in their later years. Henry and Anna Webster. Henry had been an excellent horseman and cattle raiser until his mount had stepped in a prairie dog hole and broken its leg. Henry was tossed head over teacup. The resulting injury had proven to be the end of his horseback days.

After his recovery, Flo's offer had been a lifesaver. Henry hadn't any desire to spend the rest of his days in a rocking chair. Although he favored his mended hip, the limp wasn't noticable except on days prior to a change in the weather. Anna claimed she could predict a cold front with amazing accuracy.

Anna herself was a large rawboned woman wide in the hips and built for birthing children. Her strength was an asset which was a boon to Henry and also to Florence. Lifting the heavy, food filled pots and pans was, at times, more than one could handle. Not known to the general population, Beth, the hefty barmaid, was one of Anna's middle daughters.

Florence was of average height, five foot four and slightly stocky. Her chestnut color hair, she kept rolled in a bun at the back of her neck. Her wideset green eyes framed her fine straight nose and high cheekbones. Not a beautiful nor a homely woman, but not average either. She had her finer points, but had never been described as a strikingly lovely woman.

Some would say her mouth was too wide and full, but others had refered to her as a handsome woman. Most had wondered why she hadn't married. Flo had her reasons and kept them to herself. One reason was the cross she had to bear. It was private and she had revealed it to no one. She carried the torch for one of her boarders and had done so for a number of years. Although he had never indicated he had any interest in her in any manner, Flo couldn't deny the warm rush she felt in his presence, or the outright flush she knew suffused her cheeks when he spoke to her. He was polite, but treated her with indifference as one would a sister. On the other hand, the blacksmith had tried, without success, to gain her attention.

She hadn't been cruel with her rejection of his advances. That wasn't her nature. She was very kind hearted and sensitive to other's feelings. The blacksmith had then not given up the chase. Flo disliked being part of a love triangle, but had discovered she could no more stop caring for the man of her dreams, just as the blacksmith could not stop caring for her. The course of human nature, it appeared, could no more be changed than the moon's effect on the tides of mighty oceans.

The man she pined for was, of course, Lincoln. She knew about the sad facts of his failed marriage and the loser he had chosen for a wife- the Porter girl. She was the eldest daughter of James Porter the proprietor of the only general store. Surely Linc had no idea what a wild flower she was when they married, but again nobody has the power to resist falling in love with another person when Cupid's arrow strikes its target and pierces ones heart.

The part Flo was at a loss to understand was how any woman could treat her man in the manner in which rumor had it. The wicked woman had taken up with many of the townsmen, both married and single. It hadn't mattered to her whose marriage she wrecked or how many hearts she had broken.

When poor Lincoln had really needed her comfort and aid, after his accident, she had left town with a whiskey salesman and had never been heard of again. Well, Flo thought, good riddence! But also wishing the man she cared for had not been hurt so deeply that he'd given up sharing his life with any woman. She only assumed his physical needs were taken care of by someone of the loose women he probably visited when he made his twice a month trips to Wellington under the guise of reporting to the sheriff there. He could, it appeared, handle a relationship with no promise of a commitment.

Oh, if Linc only knew of the many nights he'd been the object of Flo's dreams, he would realize how much she really cared for him. She wished, in her heart, that things could be different. Her thoughts were interupted as Anna called from the kitchen,

"I need your help, Missy." The older woman declared, *"We need to move the kettle off the range."*

Flo hurried back to the kitchen and grabbed a couple of pot holders. They each took a handle and moved the heavy iron kettle onto the table. Flo took a long handled spoon and dipped a taste of the spicey mixture. It contained taters, onions, cabbage, carrots, diced beef, and a cut up bunch of celery. It tasted just a bit flat. She scooped up a handful of salt and dropped it into the mixture and then added a few more peppercorns. Stirring the stew she then took another taste. Yes, now the stew had reached the perfection she insisted on.

Flo left the kitchen to Anna and began to set up the large dining hall. Fifty plates, cups, saucers, sets of silver, water tumblers, salt and pepper shakers, sugar bowls and pie plates.

She mentally checked off the desert list. Apple cobbler, cherry and peach pies, white cake with sugared topping and her own favorite, pickled crab apples with cloves and cinnamon sticks. She glanced at the wall clock. It was five-forty five and everything was coming together right on time. She loved it when everything turned out like this and she was positive Anna had gottenn the knack now so everything was ready at the same time. Part of her success was due to the fact she insisted on hardwood fires in the range, knowing they gave a more even heat to the iron monster.

She began filling the water tumblers from the tall pitchers. Cold water it was. Flo had, had a well drilled out back of the boardinghouse. The well driller had struck limerock at twenty feet and was willing to call that good enough.

"No way, Mister, you keep on drilling!" she had insisted.

The man had been reluctant and had explained it was going to cost a premium to go deeper. Flo had insisted and stood firm with her conviction. The man had shrugged and gone back to his drilling rig. After the disagreeable chore of punching through the limerock and finally struck sandstone the drilling became easier. Then below the sandstone he had found what she had suspected all along. Sweet, clear, cold water and even after a long, hot, Kansas summer the water still pumped up cold and clear. As far as Flo was concerned, it had been worth the extra time and effort. Florence gazed all along the tables to make sure she hadn't forgotten anything. All was in order.

The clock struck six and Flo's customers began to file in. She stood near the door and collected sixty-five cents from each patron. This was higher than the average supper usually cost, but she had discovered no one had minded paying a bit extra for her excellent meals.

"Beef stew night, Miss Florence? I thought I could smell it from across the street." Cummins, the blacksmith smiled and handed her a half dollar, a dime and a nickel. *"Dance at the Grange Hall Saturday night. May I escort you, Miss Florence?"* Cummins wasn't very hopeful.

"Sorry, Dan." She smiled, briefly.

"I know, I know, you're still pinin' for someone, but he ain't never gonna give you a tumble. Why don't you come along with me to the dance hall and have a good time anyhow?" He ask, but knew the futility of it.

After the evening meal and the tables had been cleared, Flo sat tired, but satisfied at the counter sorting out the paper money and coins. It came to thirty one dollars and twenty cents. Three of her regular customers hadn't shown up. One stranger from the hotel, who had looked her over rather thoroughly, when he stood in line, seemed as though he was about to speak, but then something had changed his mind. She wondered why he hadn't spoken. Was it something about the expression on her face, or the look in her eyes? she wondered.

She dismissed it as a mystery she would probably never solve.

The Hebers, an older couple, who had been regulars at the evening meals weren't there. She had heard they planned on making a trip to Kansas City or Omaha and figured thats where they had gone today. What worried her most was the fact Lincoln wasn't there and that wasn't like him. In the background the clatter of dishes and the jingle of silverware came from the kitchen where Henry and Anna were finishing up the wash and dry chores.

Florence totaled up the week's take and it added up to one hundred nineteen dollars and some change. Not all that bad for four days work. She wondered, at times, if serving meals on the weekends, in the dining hall, would be a wise decision, but then it would mean more work and really more than the three of them could handle. As it was, at the present time, she had full control over the quality of the food she served and taking on the extra days might change all of that without enough time to keep it all sorted out.

It would mean rising before dawn on Saturdays and Sundays and working the whole days through. She didn't mind the work, but feared the quality of the food might suffer. It was something to think about, maybe for the future. She locked up her cashbox and went to the kitchen to see how the couple was doing with the cleanup chores. Henry had already left and Anna was hanging the dish towels up to dry.

Florence poured herself a cup of coffee and carried it back to the counter out front. As she sat relaxed, she thought about Lincoln and wondered if she was ever in his thoughts. How long would she pine for him? Most probably until there was absolutly no hope of romance. At least forever and a day.

"Miss Florence?"

She raised her head from her folded arms, not remembering having fallen asleep at her counter. It was Lincoln, hat in hand.

"Ah am sorry tuh be late. Is there any beef stew left? I had a meeting with a Federal marshal." Lincoln was apologetic.

"Let me check, Lincoln, I believe there may be and some apple cobbler. I know there is some coffee left." Flo hurried to the

kitchen. There was a dollop of stew, a dab of apple cobbler and a smidgin of coffee left in the pot on the back of the big iron range. She returned to the dining hall where Lincoln still stood at the counter. *"Sit at the table and rest yourself, Lincoln."* She urged, knowing about his crooked leg and wanting him to be as comfortable as possible.

"Ah don't want tuh be no bother, Miss Florence."

He smiled, but then took a seat at the nearest table. She set the plates and mug of coffee on front of him, and then sat down across from him.

'Bother me?' her face softened as she daydreamed. *'Oh, Lincoln, if you only knew how much you do bother me. Can't you hear my heart pounding? Can't you feel the heat radiating from my body? Can't you see how flustered I get when you are near? Look up and see how flushed my face is. Oh Lincoln, I love you with all of my heart and soul. I can't help myself and I will carry my torch of love until the day I draw my last breath, come what may. Can't you see it, can't you tell, Lincoln?'*

Lincoln paused with a forkful of cobbler halfway to his mouth and was peering into her eyes in the dim light. Had he read her thoughts? she puzzled. Surely she hadn't spoken aloud, or had she?

"What is it Lincoln?" she asked as he continued to stare into her eyes with a quizical expression on his face. He put his fork back down on the pieplate and smiled.

"Ah never realized, until now, with the lampglow surrounding your fine hair an' the sparkle in your eyes, what a fine looking woman you are with those strands of hair that have come loose and are hanging down." He seemed mesmerized, *"No, don't try to push your hair back in place."* He begged, as her hand reached without thought to redo her fallen tresses.

"An' your eyes are so green. Why is it, Ah wonder, Ah never

noticed before?" Lincoln was surprised at the words he had just uttered. He had blurted out and was speaking with his heart not with conscience thought. Was this what his heart was telling him? Would she think him foolish and laugh at his words? No...there was a soft dreamy look about her face and an endearing smile graced her pretty mouth. He pondered.

Florence was a comely woman and he had known that for a long time, but it seemed as though her beauty had grown in just these last few minutes. Lincoln couldn't deny the fact that when he had been close to her lately he had felt somewhat different as though she had become part of his everyday life he had grown accostumed to. No...this was somehow different.

There had seemed to be something cold and hard in the center of his chest. Something that had formed there when his wife had been so open about her cheating ways.

Nearly like she had taken pleasure in hurting him. Right now, at this moment, this lump that had lain coldly in his chest, like a stone he toted there, had softened and felt like a lump of ice melting. He believed it had begun to soften and he didn't feel so protective of his emotions.

It was odd. He'd known Florence ever since he had been appointed as deputy here in Mayfield and needed a place to room, but here, tonight, at this place and time, he'd really taken an intimate look at Florence and something had happened. Something old as time itself that had been happening to people, at one time or another, in their lives.

The lucky ones grabbed for the brass ring and held on for dear life. Could it be? he wondered, that this was their moment in time? He sincerely hoped he would live to find out. Lincoln reached across the table and took her hand in his. Florence looked down and a tear formed and trickled down her cheek. Could this really be happening, or was she asleep and dreaming. The warmth of his hand felt real to her. Her emotions were in turmoil. It must be real, it had to be real. Here was Lincoln holding her hand and staring into her eyes. To her, there was his heart, open and expanding with what she believed was his love for her. She had hoped, but never believed this moment would come. Florence stood and rushed around to Linc's side of the table. Lincoln stood and embraced her in his arms. To Florence this is where she wanted to spend the rest of her life. She felt so safe and comfortable in his embrace. She touched his lips gently with hers and her gentle kiss was returned.

Florence looked into his eyes. *"Am I dreaming?"*

"No Florence, this is real. Ah feel your heart beating. Ah feel your body pressed close tuh me. Ah want to be near you. Ah want to make you mine. Duh you feel it too?" Linclon hugged her close. Anna would be happy if she had seen this exchange, knowing how much she cared for him. Florence thought. She wanted this embrace to last forever, but being practical, she knew this was unrealistic. She gave Lincoln a final hug and stepped back.

"Lincoln, you will never know how much I have wanted this to happen. How many nights you've been in my dreams. So many times I wanted to tell you, but I was cautious knowing how you have avoided any contact with women. Being aggressive and bold is not my way and I would have waited for you an eternity. Now I have to ask, will you be mine forever?"

Lincoln pondered her question and mulled it over in his mind. Did he love this woman, or was it too soon to tell? He did, of course, have strong emotional feelings. His love had been spurned and scorned by his first wife to whom he had poured his love out to and would have died for. He was cautious, but this fragile bloom of a new romance was something to be nurtured and developed. Florence was waiting for an answer.

"This is all new tuh me, but mah heart tells me yes Ah do love you. Let us develop this relationship slowly and make it uh lasting one." He smiled.

To Florence this was the answer she needed to hear. He was still doubtful and she could understand that. Knowing his first experience had been heartrending and it would take him time to learn to trust her completely.

"I know where my heart is and you will find I am a one man woman. You, Lincoln, are that man for now and forever. You go to

sleep tonight and keep in mind that I love you and have for a long time."

Lincoln smiled and after giving her hand a final squeeze turned and left the dining hall. With a light and happy heart, Florence cleared the table and took the plates and silver to the kitchen. She knew her dreams were becoming real and her heart told her that she had made the right decision in waiting these years for Lincoln.

FRIDAY

Chapter 5

Dawn arrived wet, and dripping. Streaky lightning flickered in the still darkened southwestern sky. The mutter of distant thunder awoke Lincoln from probably the best night's sleep he had experienced in a long time. His room in the boarding house faced west and he left the single window open to hopefully catch what fitful breeze he could. The rain had been gentle, but steady throughout much of the night.

Lincoln rolled over on his other side, back to the window, to try and catch another forty winks. The lightning appeared to be moving away and wouldn't effect Mayfield with its violent flash and crash. He fell asleep again quickly.

When he awoke again, the sun was up and the rain was only a memory, with reminders laying in small puddles. He arose and washed quickly.

He dressed in clean clothes and then checked his long barreled Colt six-gun. His life could depend on its proper function. He unloaded the cylinder and checked each cartridge. Satisfied with the visual inspection he reloaded and checked the action of the Colt.

Lincoln picked up his hat and limped down the staircase to the dining hall where Anna was serving breakfast. Ham, eggs, hotcakes and plenty of hot coffee. He attacked his food in silence barely noticing the fine texture of the ham, or that the eggs were fixed his favorite way, crispy around the edges.

As he chewed, his mind focused on the events that would occupy this busy day. If the marshal was correct in his assumption, today the bankbuster would strike and logic told him Friday would be the most likely time for it to happen. He wondered, as most men would, if he would live to see sundown. He was helpless to change anything as far as his gunplay was concerned. The style had been set years ago and accuracy above speed would be his only chance. That along with surprise. The outlaw would know, without a doubt in his mind, he had his routine down pat and had gotten away with it many times before. Lincolns appearence into the scene would give him pause and just might be the edge Lincoln would need. He didn't agree with the marshals lone hand play. He knew how the best laid plans have a way of taking an unexpected turn at a most crucial time. On the otherhand, the marshal had vast experience and seemed to know Choates by reputation. Burns should, in all probabilities, have it under control. Yet a smidgen of doubt always crept into his mind about the whole situation.

Lincoln was enjoying his second mug of coffee and looked up to find that Anna was clearing off the table. He was the last customer in the dining hall. It was strange. He'd been lost in a world of thoughts and hadn't noticed anyone leave.

"Anna, how are you this morning? Nice rain we had wasn't it?" He greeted the older woman.

"Gettin' by Mr. Lincoln. This cool damp weather makes my joints ache, but the sun is shinin' now so maybe it'll get better as the day passes. Missy was wonderin' iffin you was going to sleep all day. Yer always up at the first streak of dawn." Anna stood across from him at the table.

Linc was curious and asked her a question. *"Anna, tell me why yuh always refer tuh Miss Florence as 'Missy?'"*

The woman was silent for a time, it seemed to him. Then her face took on a sad expression and a tear trickled down her careworn cheek.

"Mr Lincoln, we done raised a passle of kids, my man and me. Four fine strappin' sons and three healthy daughters. Ah birthed four daughters, but the last little tyke Ah had when Ah was forty-seven years old. She was a sickly baby. I remember her so thin and pale in her little crib. It seemed she was all big brown eyes. She cried a lot, that Gracie child, an' couldn't gain much weight like mah other babies did." Another tear rolled down Anna's cheek. *"God called her home afore she saw her first birthday. Although we had a housefull of younguns, Ah missed that baby somthin' awful. It seemed a part of me died too. When Miss Florence hired us on, to help out, somehow, in mah mind, Ah adopted her as that little girl Ah couldn't raise. Ah had called thet little tyke 'Missy.' Well, sir, at first I tried to correct*

myself, but it kept happenin' so often, it just become uh habit ah couldn't break." The woman stood with hands folded.

Linc was moved and felt uncomfortable. He felt sympathy for the woman and her loss. He wish he had never asked, as it was like opening up an old wound that would have been better left healed.

"Anna, Ah had no idea. Ah am so sorry."

She stood in silence, just letting memories wash over her. Hoping little Gracie was happy in Heaven and looking down on her old maw once in a while. She knew how Lincoln felt and tried to ease his discomfort.

"Ah know yuh didn't know, so don't let ut bother yuh none an' just let ut pass. When yuh reach my age, your life will be filled with memories and Ah do hope you will be able to look back along the years and have the good times stack up much higher than the sad times. You know, though, the Good Lord has planned out each of our lives and there ain't really much a body kin do tuh change things," Anna replied.

"Where is Miss Florence this morning?" Linc inquired.

"She was about earlier whilst you were eatin' but now she's done left for the farm where she gits her eggs, vegetables, meat and fruit. She always goes on Fridays an' probably won't git back until near three, four o'clock."

Lincoln was relieved to hear that and hadn't realized he'd been holding his breath. Anna seemed to want to say more as she stood in hesitation.

"Mr Lincoln, Missy would scalp me alive if she knew Ah had tole you this, but yuh know she has been sweet on yuh fer a long spell?" Anna seemed quite serious.

If it had been yesterday, Linc would have been surprised, as Florence had either kept her feelings well hidden, or he hadn't paid enough mind to the world around him. The social part of his life he had abandoned when Marie had left town with the whiskey salesman.

He knew he had more or less ignored everything but what was connected with keeping the law. He had believed she and the blacksmith were an item as they had sat together in church and carried on what appeared to be spirited conversations in the dining hall. He had decided long ago a woman wasn't going to be part of his life. One heartbreak had been a lesson well learned. Of course, their conversation last night, and the fact that Florence was beginning to occupy a major part of his waking thoughts, left him in a quandry.

Law enforcement and cattle working were the limit of his experience as far as making a living were concerned. Mayfield being a small town, there wasn't a constant danger by being a deputy sheriff. When the time came to hang up his gun, he would, of course, be too old to work cattle anymore. If he did indeed live to see the sunset, some more serious considerations, on his part, would have to be thought about in depth.

"Anna, take care an' stay off the streets after dinner. There will most certainly be lead flyin'" Linc warned.

"Ah'll keep thet in mind, Mr Lincoln. You consider what Ah have revealed tuh yuh, but please never say anything to Missy." Anna cleared the dishes and coffee mug off the table and wiped the oilcloth clean.

Lincoln had promised to take a look at some fence cutting and most probably cattle rustling that had taken place at Simpson's Circle S ranch which was about an hours ride southwest of town. If he started now, he could be back just about noontime. There was little he could do about the rustler problem, but he wanted to warn the rancher not take matters into his own hands. Catching the rustlers red handed was, of course a different matter all together and justice was swift.

Experience told him holdups occured between two-thirty and four in the afternoons, for the most part, with few exceptions. Most of the days business had been conducted and the cash box was likely to be full just before the bank closed at four.

He walked to the livery barn where he kept his two horses. One was a plain brown gelding that could lope all day, if needed and live off the land. The other a spirited, shiney, black with three white stockings and a nearly perfect triangle of white on its forehead between its eyes. The black horse was fast, but didn't have the stamina or fortitude for a long run like the brown horse did.

Lincoln wanted to take the brown horse, but was dismayed to find a shoe had worked loose on his forehoof. He wouldn't have time to have the smith re-nail it and still make the afternoon deadline. He reluctantly returned the brown horse to his stall and then saddled the black. After leading the horse out of the livery barn, he mounted and rode southwest out of Mayfield. He noticed, at once, how humid the day had become. He kept the horse at a slow trot and stayed on the wagonwheel rutted trail that would lead past the Circle S ranch.

Later he pulled up beneath a large, stately elm tree that grew along the trail. Some of the limbs were dead and the massive trunk was scarred by an old lightning strike. It offered a place to rest his horse and let him cool off for a spell. Linc dismounted and dropped the reins. He removed his Stetson and wiped a sleeve across his forehead. Scanning the horizon in all directions, it appeared he was the only traveler at this time. Florence, in his mind, appeared as a daydream. Her smile, the way her hair had come loose and curled across her forehead, the way her eyebrows had arched as he had professed what was in his heart last night. He wondered, would he live to see her face again? To feel the warm caress and the beating of her heart as he held her? Only the Good Lord knew. Setting his hat back on he mounted his horse and trotted away.

Soon Simpson's outbuildings appeared on the horizon and Linc was relieved as his bum leg was beginning to ache from the long ride. Thirty wasn't old by any means, but he worried about how long he could support himself after he could no longer ride a horse. He'd attempted to get a loan from Rawlind, the towns miserly banker, but had been turned down. He had wanted to buy a piece of land that lay North of Mayfield. The section he had his eye on was privately owned. He knew it was overpriced, but it was what he wanted. A recent inquiry told him it was still for sale and the price had been lowered just a tad. Somehow he would find a way to aquire it, somehow.

Linc approached the ranch and dismounted to open the gate.

After leading his horse through he carefully closed and latched it. Re-mounting he rode to the bunkhouse where he supposed Simpson would be as he'd known Linc was coming before lunchtime.
He had guessed wrong as Simpson came loping up from the barn, mounted on a piebald mare he was in the habit of riding around the ranch.

"Howdy, Linc, you get any of that rain over yon, or did Mayfield stay dry and dusty?" The man greeted him.

"Mornin' Simpson, Ut did rain fer a spell sometime last night, but had cleared when Ah got up. Lets have uh look at that fence thats been cut."

They both rode along exchanging small talk about ranching, cattle prices, the bitter winter they had endured and the hefty barmaid at the Longbranch Saloon. Simpson was a single man who had never married and Linc felt the man was wise to stay away from the heartbreak of a busted romance. They came to a long stretch of barbwire was missing and a fence post was pulled from the ground. Linc examined the end of the cut wire and correctly determined it had indeed been cleanly snipped with a large pair of side cutters.

"How many head of cows duh yuh figger are missin', Simpson?" He asked.

"Bout twenty-five head I venture. It ain't a whole lot each time, but this is twice this month." The rancher answered.

The tracks lead south and anyone with a suspicious mind would naturally suspect Simpson's neighbor. There was no use in speculation though until more evidence could be gathered. Linc had learned, through the years, that jumping to conclusions often left a feller with egg on his face or at least one foot in his mouth. Just plodding along slowly and taking one's time to examine all the facts, caught more thieves in the long run.

"Let's foller them tracks fer a while, Simpson, and see where they lead. Ah've noticed somethin' pecular about one of the horses

thet was used here. He's got a shoe missin' on his left hind hoof." Linc stated.

"Humph, I never noticed that. How did you see that after last nights rain?" Simpson wondered.

"Some of the things a feller learns tuh pay attention tuh over the years." He told the rancher.

"Linc, you suppose we should get some of the boys to ride along, just in case we run into a bunch of rustlers?"

"Won't be necessary. If memory serves, these tracks are heading right for that wash and if thats the case they will be all washed away by last nights rain and the rush of the water in the dry creek bed."

They followed the tracks until they became lost in the hard stoney wash. Although they trotted along both sides of the wash, they didn't find any more sign. Discourged, they returned to the ranch. Linc told Simpson he would comb a wider area, check with the blacksmith for a pony with three shoes and listen to the local gossip. That was about all he could do for the present.

"Tell yuh Linc, if me and the boys ever catch those rustlers red-handed, there ain't gonna be nothing for you to do. As we're going to have a necktie party at the nearest tree!" Simpson sounded frustrated and angry.

"If it ever comes tuh pass, Simpson, bury them deep an' don't ever let me know 'bout ut. Yuh know what Ah'd have tuh do. The lawless days is about over." Linc warned his friend.

Simpson knew what the lawman meant. The West just wasn't the same as it had been a few years ago and a man would have to watch himself very carefully. They parted and Linc began his trip back to Mayfield.

As he trotted along his eyes were drawn to a group of circling buzzards above a small grove of trees. It was nearly a half mile from the wagon trail. Either they hadn't been there when he had ridden out, or they had been circling an area of the sky where the sun had hidden them. He trotted cross country until he reached the edge of the grove. His nose told him whatever had attracted the buzzards, wasn't any creature that could be counted amoung the living.

He moved into the trees and discovered the remains of what had once been a black horse. The buzzards had done their work well and he couldn't determine the sex, or what had killed the horse. He did file away one vital piece of information though. The shoe was missing off the left hind hoof.

A quick check of the immediate area didn't reveal any signs of a new grave, but the possibility that Simpson had indeed caught the rustlers at work, existed and a closer check of this area when he wasn't strapped for time would be a must.

Linc left the grove of trees and continued toward Mayfield. A few minutes from town he met Abe Thompson driving his work wagon full of supplies toward his ranch that was situated further southwest than Simpson's. He stopped and waited until Thompson pulled up beside him.

"Hi, Abe." He greeted the man.

"Hey, Lincoln." The man replied with a grin.

"Abe have you been bothered by rustlers like your neighbor Simpson has?" Linc asked him.

"Matter of fact I have lost a few head, but not enough to bother you about." Abe seemed a bit nervous and evasive.

"Well yuh know where tuh find me iffin it does become a problem." Linc said as he rolled and lit a smoke. Thompson nodded and slapped his horses with the reins.

Linc arrived back in Mayfield near one-thirty and knew he wouldn't have time to eat. He tied his horse behind the jail and entered the back door of his office. One of the flies had won the head-butting contest and was lying on its back, with legs folded. The other was lazily crawling up the window pane, searching for a new game partner.

He debated on taking one of the Winchester model '94 30/30s out of the gun rack, but decided to wait until things began to develop and he could discover how the holdup would be conducted. He could observe the entire bank building from the window of his office. At the present time he detected nothing unusual. There was only the normal business in and out of the front door.

He hoped Anna and her husband had taken his warning seriously and would keep to the boarding house until the holdup was history. His thoughts turned briefly to Florence and his new attitude toward her. The glow of her eyes in the lamplight, how the few strands of hair, that had escaped, hung down, seemed to have a lighter color than the rest. The shape of her face and how her expression had changed when he had expressed what was in his heart. He shook his head to clear it. He needed to concentrate on the present situation.

Linc glanced at the wall clock and was amazed to discover it was two forty-five. He turned to gaze out the window and found he'd nearly missed the opening scene. A cowboy riding a horse and leading another pony, picked his way furtively between the buildings. He was working his way toward the rear of the bank. The celebration was about to begin.

He left the rifle in the rack and turned to leave by the rear door. His knee gave out and he fell to the floor. The pain was brief, but the ache would stay with him a few days. He picked himself up and hobbled toward the rear of the bank.

There was no sign of the marshal and he had to assume he was in the bank somewhere. Linc skirted the buildings until he could see the cowboy holding the reins of both horses. Linc carefully and quietly stalked the man until he was near enough to touch him. The cowboy bent his head to cupped hands, lighting a cigarette he had rolled. Linc drew his Colt and did his best to bend the barrel of it over the man's head.

Without a grunt the man dropped to the ground, unconscious. After looking about and seeing nobody, Linc dragged the limp dude behind a shed and returned for the horses. He led them to the shed also and tied their reins to the hasp on the door.

Taking time to rope and tie the man he'd knocked out, he returned to a spot at the rear of the bank where he could see, but couldn't be seen and waited for 'Molly Malone' to make a withdrawl from the bank. He wanted to light up a cheroot, but concentrating on the action that was about to unfold was his most critical job at the present time.

It wasn't a long wait. He heard two shots fired inside the bank. In no time at all, it seemed, the phony old gal hurried in the direction of the back alley behind the bank. He turned his head this way and that frantically looking for his horse and partner. He'd pulled off the wig and was struggling with the dress.

"Partner, yer man just left with the two horses." Linc called.

Choates looked around, dropping his large handbag, and drew his gun. Lordy, but the man was fast! He fired twice before Linc had his gun lined up. One shot hit him in the lower right side, and spoiled his aim. Linc held his six-shooter with both hands and pulled the trigger. He never heard the third shot the dying man aimed in his direction. The bullet hit his head before the sound reached his ears.

It was a blinding white flash of shock and Linc was knocked to the ground. The townspeople were reacting to the sound of shots fired, in and around the bank. In the lobby they found the teller wounded by a stray shot the marshal had fired in reaction as he died. Rawlind confirmed that the disguised hold up artist had spun and fired at the marshal, when asked to surrender. That bullet had ended the marshal's life.

Out back they discovered the bank robber dead with Lincoln's bullet through his heart and it had shattered his spine on the way out. Linc was lying in the dust, gun in hand and bleeding from his two wounds. The last bullet fired by the now dead outlaw, had plowed a furrow across the top of his head. Linc still showed signs of life by the shallow, short, gasping breaths.

Doc Hutchinson had Linc carried to his office and prepared to do everything in his power to save the popular deputy's life. Doc had been a surgeon in the last stages of the Civil War and had treated many bullet wounds then and after he'd taken up practice in this frontier town. The body wound wasn't going to be fatal, he discovered, as he was probing for the bullet. There were no vital organs involved in that area next to the hip. Baring infection Linc would recover from that wound. The head wound was probably the most dangerous of the two.

Doc wondered if Lincoln would ever recover from the coma he was now lost in. If he did, would he recognize any of his friends? He had seen this type of wound before and he didn't hold much hope. He cleaned the head wound and bound it up, hoping for the best.

Stand By Me
Chapter 6

Florence drew the wagon to a halt in front of the boarding-house. After climbing down, she tied the horse to the hitchrack. It had been a tiring and bumpy ride, but she had accomplished what she'd set out to do. All the supplies for next weeks menu were piled in the wagon. A side of beef, potatoes, onions, carrots, some early sweet corn. A sack of flour, ten pounds of salt, ten pounds of sugar, some late season ruhbarb were amoung the supplies. She had no sooner stepped up on the veranda when a frantic Anna met her at the door.

"Missy, yore man has got shot up. He tole me this mornin' tuh stay off the streets an' then he's the one who got hurt... He's over at Doc Hutchinsons. He's unconscious at the last report. My mister just come from there." Anna broke the news as best she could.

The shock of the news knocked all the strength out of Florence. Her knees gave out and she sat down hard on the front steps. She dropped her head into her hands. With heart thudding and a numb feeling sweeping over her, she began to weep.

"Oh, Lincoln, Ah feared something like this would happen. Why, Lord, oh why after we just found each other?" She murmered between sobs.

"Missy, he ain't dead, go to him. Ah'll take care of the supplies an' get the supper meal done." Anna gripped her shoulder. *"You need to be strong for Mister Lincoln, he needs your strength most of all right now."*

Florence knew Anna was right. Her place was with Lincoln and Anna could handle the supper meal with her husbands help. She stood and wiped her eyes. Her heart told her to rush to the Doc's office, but her body wouldn't respond. She walked slowly, dreading what she had to do. She wasn't prepared for the sight of Lincoln lying so still with his head wrapped in white. Florence considered herself fairly tough, being of pioneer stock, but as the blood rushed from her brain and the room began to spin she sighed and folded into a heap on the floor.

Doc Hutchinson straightened her out, raised her feet higher than her head and covered her with a blanket. She would come out of it in due time.

Slowly the world came back into focus as her eyes fluttered and opened.

"What happened, Doc?" She was confused.

"You just fainted, Florence. You'll be ok in a minute or two. Just lie there a little longer until you feel better."

"Is Lincoln going to be alright?" She questioned, looking up at Doc.

"I'll be honest with you, girl, it could go either way. What he needs is bed rest and somebody to feed him three times a day." Doc explained.

"I'm willing, Doc, I love that man. Just get him moved to his room at the boarding house and I'll take care of him."

"Ah got tuh warn you, Florence, he may not know yuh if and when he ever comes outa his coma." Doc advised. He was being frank with her.

"Makes no nevermind. Just have him brought over. You don't know how much I love this man." Florence picked herself up off the floor. She bent over and kissed Lincoln's dry lips.

Doc was naturally touched. Florence was the daughter he never had and he felt very protective of her. He left the office and soon returned with three other men. They carefully carried the wounded man to Florence's boardinghouse and up the stairs to his room. Florence did everything she could do to make him comfortable in his bed. She stood looking down at him, wishing there was something more she could do. It would take time and there were no assurances he would live through the night.

Lincoln was hardy and had an exceptionally strong will to live. Florence slept on a cot in the same room. She was startled awake twice, during the night, when Linc's breathing had become ragged and seemed to stop. Both times she had leapt from her cot, heart pounding, and had shaken the unconcious man. This was apparently the proper thing to do, as his breathing had settled down to a regular, steady pace again.

Florence was tired and cranky the next day, but it had been a labor of love. Anna understood well knowing what was involved caring for a sick loved one. As the days passed, Florence divided her time between the running of the boardinghouse and caring for Linc. Not that her business suffered. She still took the same pains to assure that the meals were wholesome, the ingredients choice and the food she served was tasty. It was much extra work, but Florence seemed to thrive on it.

For the next ten days there didn't appear to be any change in Lincoln's condition. When she brought him his broth at noon he would be lying in exactly the same position she had left him in that morning. The same held true in the evenings. Florence fretted about this and finally checked with Doc Hutchinson.

"Ah warned yuh not tuh expect too much." Doc shook his head. *"Give it a few more days. The blow tuh his head has been a shock tuh his system and it takes time for things tuh beginning working proper and on their own again. The fact that he has made it this far is encourging."* Doc gave her a hug. *"Be hopeful, Florence."*

She wasn't satisfied, but had to rely on Doc's knowledge and experience. What would she do, she wondered, if God called her loved one home? After he had admitted his caring for her, she had fallen deeply in love.

Six days later she found him lying on his right side in the morning. This was encourging as it was the first time he had moved on his own. The whole day seemed brighter and her tasks easier. Henry was first to notice how much more cheerful she was that morning and commented on it.

"Good news this mornin' Florence?" he asked.

"He rolled over sometime during the night and really that's the first sign of progress he's shown." Florence explained with a bright smile. It was as though some of her fears had been laid to rest. In her own mind though, she know this was only a small step in his recovery.

At noon, the next day, when she entered his room with the soup, his eyes were open and he seemed to be aware of her presence. His eyes followed her movements.

"Well, Lincoln, are you back with us?" She asked, sitting on the edge of his bed.

He was pale, hollow eyed, and had two weeks growth of whiskers, as she hadn't had a barber come in to shave him. He'd lost weight and looked so wasted. He peered at her questionly and somewhat blankly. Flo's eyes began to tear. He didn't know her. *'Hold it back, Flo.'* she told herself, *'don't let him see you break down. After all it's better than just lying there.'* She was, of course, disappointed, believing he didn't recognize her. Despite her best efforts, two teardrops escaped and trickled down her cheeks. Flo turned away, hiding her disappointment and sorrow.

"Don't.....c-cry.....Miss........F-f-florence." Lincoln had spoken haltingly and each word had been an effort, but he KNEW her! She spun around and threw herself across him, the bowl of soup falling to the floor unnoticed.

"Oh, Lincoln, my love, yore gonna be well again!"

She hugged him. Lincoln clumbsily put one arm across her back and weakly returned her hug. To Lincoln, the woman in his arms was something he had yearned for without realizing what it was that had been missing from his life. She just felt right, being there. He knew now no matter how things turned out, Florence was going to be the love of his life. All the hurt and disappointment of his first love faded and slipped to an area in his mind where he stored the memories he never wanted to be reminded of again.

Florence stared into his eyes and pressed her lips to his in a tender, loving meeting of two who had found what they had been look-ing for. She was happier than she had ever been in her young life. She just knew he would get better and improve a little each day.

Lincoln realized Florence had been the one whose voice he had heard in the deep black land of his coma. His head still ached. His memory was partially blank in the area of what had happened to him, but he knew Florence could fill in the blanks he couldn't remember. It was something about Rawlind's bank, but it wasn't part of his memory.

From that day forward Lincoln seemed to improve rapidly. Soon he was sitting up and feeding himself. The next week he was taking a few hesitant steps with Florence's help. She enjoyed there sessions when she could be close to Lincoln. His balance was becom-ing better, but there were times when he nearly fell. Florence was al-ways there for him to lean on.

Florence knew he was improving as the days passed and he began asking questions.

"Has someone been feeding kitty?" He asked one evening.

"I've kept her fed and she's about to produce a litter of kit-tens. You wouldn't believe how tubby she looks." Flo smiled.

"Is the sheriff taking care of the office?"

"Yes, he stops in twice a week. He was here to see you twice when you were out of it." Florence explained.

Although it was painful, Linc worked on getting the stiffness out of his side. His fear was that it would never get limber enough for him to take up his lawman duties again and he worried about it. How would he make a living?

One day he decided to try a few steps without Florences help. As he was taking stiff and slow steps, with Florence backing ahead of him, he lost his balance and fell forward. If it hadn't been for her quick reaction, he would have landed on his face. She caught him and as they stood face to face wrapped in each others arms, Lincoln realized how good it made him feel to be holding her. Without thought, or hesi-tation he kissed her. It surprised them both and gave Florence a feeling of yearning and also being needed and wanted. This was a big step in their new romance.

ON THE MEND

Chapter 6

Through the late summer and early autumn, Lincoln continued to improve. The stiffness in his side, he realized, would never be completely gone. He practiced drawing his gun and thumbing the hammer back. To him, it didn't seem to be a slower draw, but then he had never been really fast and had concentrated more on making his first shot go where he wanted it to. He also repeatedly lifted a ten pound bag of sand that Florence had sewn up for him. As the stiffness loosened he realized he had reached a point where there wasn't going to be any more improvement.

***

He saddled his brown horse on a morning in late October and rode out of town. He stopped in a small grove of trees and tied his horse to a branch. Digging into his saddlebags and took out his Colt revolver, gunbelt and two boxes of .45 caliber ammunition. Lincoln set up a target made of a dead tree limb and paced off what he believed to be about 50 feet. Loading his gun, he practiced drawing and firing. Through the first fifty rounds he had to concentrate extra hard to even come close. This was no good. Shooting left handed was even worse. Clumbsy at the very least. Then using both hands, the left one as a brace, he began to bring back the accuracy he was used to. Satisfied, but aching, he rode back town and told Florence what he had done.

"Lincoln, you're not thinkin' of going back to your deputy job are you? I couldn't stand the thought of you facing a criminal across the sights of a gun again. I can't lose you. I don't even want to think about that possibility. We can make it with just the profits of the boardinghouse. Just lose a little bit of that he-man attitude and we can have a calm and loving life together."

"Florence, its all I know and a man must do what he must." She was unhappy with his decision, but would stand by him in any case.

On the first day of November he contacted the sheriff and reported he was ready to resume his duties. Naturally one of the first things he wanted to do was check out the area where he had found the dead horse. He rode to that spot one sunny morning and began probing some of the most likely spots in the little grove of trees. The dead horse was only bones, but he used it as a reference point. He had brought along a spade and used it.

Three hours later, after studying and digging, he unearthed some human parts. He carefully exhumed that area until he had discovered the remains of two bodies. What clothes were intact led him to believe they both had been male. The angle of the neck bones of each were at a twisted and broken angle. Surely they had been hung.

Lincoln, of course had no proof who the judge, jury and executioner had been, but would believe, for all time, it had been Simpson. The rancher who had lost a number of cows to some rustlers. In his mind he played out the scene of Simpson and his crew catching the rustlers red-handed and using swift Western justice, had indeed lynched those men on the spot. He was in a quandry. Simpson was, at heart, a good man and sometimes anyone pushed to the limit would go against his principals and do something he wouldn't usually do. He wondered if indeed the man had already caught and disposed of them only a few hours before Lincoln had checked on the fence cutting episode.

He filed this information back in his mind and knew he would have to ask Simpson about it. As he had decided, Simpson was indeed a decent man that had been pushed too far. Also the West would be better off with two less outlaws. He had deceided that there would be no charges filed against the rancher. This was Lincoln's law and he was one to bend the rules just a bit if the circumstances warrented.

Lincoln rode slowly back to town and stabled his brown horse. It was lunch time and he went to stand in line for Florence's noon meal. He sat alone at one of the long tables and his mind was filled with visions of two hanging men.

As he sipped the last of his second cup of coffee, Florence sat down across the table from him.

"Lincoln, you have something burdensome on your mind. I can see something is troubling you."

He looked up and met her piercing gaze. *"Yes, I have. I've made a decision and am going to stick by it. In the eyes of the law it would most probably be a wrong one, but it involves the welfare of a good man and my conscience wouldn't let me do what the law strictly says should be done. Also I don't have proof positive the man is surely guilty of what I believe."*

Florence understood his deep thoughts. *"I know, Lincoln, you being a fair man, you will do the right thing. As to the facts of it, I never want to know. Just do what you think is best for all concerned."* She would abide with his decision no matter how it turned out.

She loved Lincoln with all her heart. There was one question in her mind though, was Lincoln ever going to ask to become his bride? She wanted to be Lincoln's wife more than anything she had ever thought about.

"Well, Florence, I'm going to ride out an satisfy my mind about this."

He reached across the table and gave her hand a squeeze. He stood and left the dining hall. Florence had a lot on her mind and there were many unanswered questions she would really like to have answered, but it was Lincoln's law enforcing business and she would never ask.

As Lincoln rode toward the Simpson ranch, his decison was firm and he wouldn't change his mind. As he faced the man, he told him, *"Simpson, Ah found the horse with the missing shoe along with a couple uh cowboys that had been hung."*

Simpson had shuffled his feet and stared at the ground.

"As I tole you one time before, my friend, the lawless days are past. If the same situation should ever come tuh pass, yuh let the law handle ut. We'll never talk of this again." Lincoln talked sternly to the man, but wanted to impress upon him, not to take the law into his own hands again.

"Linc, Ah'll take yer advice tuh heart, an' surely thank yuh fer not actually pinin' me down on the subject."

He had as much as confessed, but as Linc had decided, the world was better off with less outlaws like the ones he'd found planted in the ground. Lincoln left Simpson's ranch and rode back to town. The leaves on what trees he could see, especially the hardwoods, were particularly bright with their autumn colors.

He wasn't fond of the coming winter. The cold and bitter days ahead would make his crippled leg ache. Then there were the two newer wounds. The one in his side probably wouldn't cause him any grief, but the one he had suffered across the top of his head was a different story. It had left a pink scar where no hair would grow. The headaches he had suffered regularly, seemed to have finally left for good. Hopefully the winter weather wouldn't bring them back.

The brown horse raised his ears and turned his head sideways. He nickered once and slowed his pace. Lincoln brought the horse to a halt and stared in the direction the horse indicated. Nearly out sight on the flat prairie, he could just make out what appeard to be a lone figure walking slowly. Lincoln turned his horse in that direction.

As he trotted toward the person, he wondered what cirstumstance had left them without a horse. Drawing near he discovered it was Fellows the bartender. The day had warmed and Fellows was carrying his sheepskin coat.

"Fellows, how is it I find you out for a stroll this fine day?" Linc asked his friend.

The man's sad looking eyes became even sadder.

"Linc, Ah am so embarrassed it pains me tuh even say. Usually when Ah travel Ah rent uh buggy from the livery, but today one of the buggys was already rented out and the hostler was repairing the other one. Ah just wanted tuh go out tuh the Matson ranch where Beth, muh barmaid, stays. Don't let ut be known, but Am sweet on thet girl. Ah never got there. Thet horse they done give me tuh ride caught me off guard and bucked me off when he done seen uh piece uh paper uh flyin' along and spooked. Tossed me behind over teacup."

"Well, my friend, climb aboard and lets trot on back tuh town. This horse kin carry both uh us." Linc smiled.

DON'T GET MAD, GET EVEN

Chapter 7

Near the middle of November, Linc, one morning after he had checked in at his office, he decided to stop at the bank and have a chat with Rawlind. He entered the bank and found he had to wait. The banker was busy foreclosing on a farm.

Lincoln sat at a solid, round, oaken table and figited. He hated waiting without purpose. As he shifted his feet over and about the floor, he was surprised when his foot discovered what seemed to be a loose board on the floor. As he carefully explored with his booted toe, he was surprised to find as he stepped on the end of the short board, the end nearest him rose. He looked down and found there was an opening about six inches wide and two feet long.

The space was empty and dusty like it hadn't been opened for many years. Even at a close examination, it was very difficult to detect that it was anything but a normal floorboard. It was hinged, but for what purpose he had no idea. It had probably been here since the bank was built before either he or Rawlind had come to this town. It didn't appear this board had been opened in all that time. Linc believed he was the only person who had discovered this. He toed the board shut and gazed about the lobby. Nobody was paying the least bit of attention to him and most probably no one had seen him open the hiding place. The faint outline of a plan began to form in Lincoln's mind. It would take a bit of thinking to perfect something that would work, but he had the time and a smile appeared on his face.

A few moments later he was ushered into Rawlind's office. The money changer sat at his impressive desk, puffing on an expensive cigar and writing something on an official looking paper. A smug, self-satisfied expression was etched on his face. Probably nothing he enjoyed more than forclosure and the fact he had so much control over the lives of his customers. Finally he looked up after making Lincoln wait for nearly five minutes. He peered down his nose at Linc and waited again for a few moments. Linc was patient, as what he was about to do gave him a secret lift.

"If you've come to beg for a loan, don't bother. You're even

more of a risk than you were before." Rawlind huffed, making the blue smoke thick around his head.

Linc was silent and just stood there making Rawlind wait. He stared into Rawlind's eyes and smiled. His plan would either let some air out of Rawlind's pride and might even burst his bubble of superiority. Finally he spoke.

"Why no, Ah jest stopped by tuh ask yuh uh question and tuh give yuh the good news." Linc explained.

The banker stared at him for a full minute and Linc could see the man was puzzled.

"What was your question?" He asked.

Lincoln shifted his weight to his good leg. *"It's common knowledge thet when Ah shot thet holdup artist, Ah probably saved your bank a lot uh money. Naturally Ah don't know the sum, but Ah'm shore yuh wouldn't want tuh lose any of ut."* Lincoln paused. *"Ah never expected tuh git uh reward fer this, but as yuh well know Ah was laid up fer the better part of three months. In all thet time yuh never stopped by tuh see how Ah was doin' er tuh even say, thanks fer savin' my bank all thet money."*

Rawlind looked uncomfortable for just a moment and shifted in his chair. He took the cigar out of his mouth.

"I intended to, but just never found the time. Anyway you shouldn't expect anything for just doing your job." He justified his actions. It was about what Linc expected.

"You are correct, Rawlind, but there are uh a multitude of colors other than black an' white an' each situation is unique. Ut's bin said 'The road to hell is paved with good intentions.'" Lincoln paused again. *"There is another proverb too. 'Yer chickens always come home tuh roost.' Don't be much surprised iffin the next robbery is much more successful. Now iffin yuh should happen tuh mention whot Ah've jest said, tuh anyone, Ah will deny ut. Even though yuh*

hold mortgages over the heads uh many uh the townspeople here, Ah believe Ah kin count on many more of them as friends. Ah doubt very much iffin you kin name three in town er surrounding, thet are friends uh yours." Linc told the man.

Rawlind was at a loss to understand what the man was driving at, but some of the things he'd said would no doubt take some thinking on. Just who did this deputy think he was talking to? Rawlind was ruffled, but managed to keep calm. Indifferently, he examined the end of his cigar.

"What news do you have, deputy. That you have gotten rid of the town lush?"

"Ah wanted to tell you, kitty had a litter of six kittens. Calico, solid gray, solid yellow, white, black, and tiger stripped orange."

Rawlind stared at him, wondering had he stepped off the edge of reality? He watched as Lincoln left his office. The man appeared to have lost touch and would bear watching. Rawlind noticed his hands were shaking and he hid them under his desk. Linc left the bank feeling much better. Surely he'd made that pompus ass believe he was nuts. It was all part of the plan he had begun to formulate in his mind. He walked to the general store and browsed until he found what he needed. He purchased a thin brief case, some writing paper, envelopes, and two pencils. Rawlind was going to be one sorry individual after Linc finished what he had planned. On the other side of the street and down near the corner, there was a gunsmith who had a small shop there.

Linc crossed the street just behind a freight wagon loaded with barrels and kegs. He entered the gunsmith shop and gazed at the revolvers on display in the glass cased counter. He didn't find what he was seeking. The gunsmith stood patiently waiting for Linc to make up his mind.

"Lookin fer uh two shot Derringer in .41 caliber, Mr Mills, an' Ah don't see one here." Linc explained.

"I have one that was left here for repair more than a year

ago and never claimed. Believe it was owned by a passing whiskey salesman. It isn't the most popular gun ever manufactured, you know, and I don't have any call for them, but it is an excellent choice for the use in which it was intended. I have repaired it and have test fired it out back, so I'm sure it is reliable." Mills explained.

"Les have uh look see." Linc asked.

The smith opened one of the drawers on his workbench and returned to the counter with the gun. Linc took it from him and opened the action, releasing the catch and tipping the barrels up to look through them. It was what he wanted.

"How much yuh askin' fer ut, Mills?" He wondered.

"They're worth $25 dollars new, but as you can see this gun has some wear and the bill for the repair is three dollars ninety cents. Let me see, hmmmm...If you will give me half the price of a new gun, $12.50, then the gun is yours." Mills answered.

"Sounds reasonable iffin yuh will toss in a box of bullets then we've made uh deal." Linc offered.

Mills reached into the display case and took a box of Remington Kleenbores from the supply there. Linc paid for his purchases and left the gunsmith's shop.

Shortly after the noon lunch, when Linc retuned to the bank, he wasn't dressed in his working clothes. He had on his Sunday best, tie and all. He had left his six-gun, holster and badge at the boardinghouse. There was only one customer at the teller's cage so Linc waited. When the customer had left he stepped up to the cage, drew his Derringer, pointed it at the teller and ask for all the money he had. The man frantically darted his eyes about the room, but finding no help, he complied.

"Don't yell, er Am gonna blow some new holes in yuh." Linc warned.

The teller, who had been wounded in the summer holdup, didn't care to be shot again. He handed it all across the counter and ducked below the counter edge. Linc opened his new briefcase, and stuffed all the bills on top of the writing paper, closed the case, tipped his hat and calmly strolled to the little oaken table, his back to the teller. Putting his briefcase on the tabletop, he smiled to himself. Rawlind was going to make a fool of himself and Linc was going to be so innocent.

His back to the teller and out of sight he opened his briefcase, toed the secret floorboard open, dumped the money and his Derringer in and closed the board. Linc heard a commotion behind him. He smiled to himself. He removed a sheet of paper and a pencil from his briefcase and began to write. *'Dear Charlie....'*

"Turn around, Lincoln, you didn't think you could get away with it, did you?" It was Rawlind.

Lincoln turned around and found the banker pointing a gun at him. He put down his pencil and raised his hands.

"This is the first time, I believe, a banker has held up one of his customers." Linc grinned.

"It's in his briefcase," the excited teller brayed, wringing his hands. Rawlind watched Linc closely as he opened the briefcase, still pointing the gun at him.

"What are yuh lookin' fer Rawlind?" Linc asked seemingly puzzled.

"The money you took, of course!" the banker barked. Some customers were milling about, curious as to what in the world was going on.

"A'm sorry, but Ah have no idea what in the world you're babblin' about." Linc replied innocently.

The newly appointed town marshal arrived and tried to find out what was going on.

"Search this man. He just held up my teller!" Rawlind barked angrily.

"This is the deputy sheriff, Mr Rawlind." The marshal said. *"Sorry, Lincoln, he insists."*

Lincoln just shrugged and told the marshal to go ahead. The marshal complied even to the extent of ripping out the lining of the briefcase and searching Lincoln thourghly.

"Mister Rawlind there's no money or gun here." He stared at the banker suspiciously.

"Ah come in here just tuh do some business an' whilst Ah was waitin' Ah set here tuh write uh letter. Next thing Ah knowed, Rawlind here comes uh running over an' wavin' his gun in mah face claimin' Ah robbed him. What Ah think is thet he's paranoid ever since thet robbery last summer an' he sees bad guys uh crawlin' outa the woodwork." Linc grinned.

"Mister Rawlind, this man don't have your money, yuh shore yuh didn't imagine the whole thing?" The marshal was puzzled.

"He robbed my bank! Search him again! I don't know how he did it and made the gun and money disappear, but sure as I'm standing here, he robbed my bank!" Rawlind was becoming frantic which didn't help his cause any.

The town marshal searched Linc carefully again and of course didn't find anything. Then he opened the drawer on the oaken table and looked underneith. He told Linc to go.

"I can't hold this man without any evidence." He explained.

Rawlind was livid and shaking with pent up anger. He would have to make up the losses himself whether it was a dollar or a million. He knew he'd been robbed. How that crippled up, gimpy, sleepy eyed, dull witted, deputy had done it... he would never know. After a careful accounting, when the bank closed, he discovered there was close to $1,100 dollars missing.

Over the next few cold weeks, Lincoln entered and left the bank with his briefcase, making deposits for Florence. Dear Florence. He'd grown to love her more with each passing day. He smiled at Rawlind each chance he had. Just to let the miserly man know he'd been had and couldn't prove it. He could feel Rawlind's eyes burning holes in his back each time he left the bank.

Lincoln never took the money, or the gun out of the secret space in the floor. It remained in the bank. You could say the robbery never really happened. Linc was, in reality, innocent of taking any money out of the bank.

He did, though, draw his $2700 dollars out and buy the parcel of land he admired. He laughed as he recalled the expression on the banker's face when he told him, *"Ah don't wanta leave my money in uh bank thets always gettin' robbed."*

Lincoln and Florence were married later, just before Christmas and lived out their happy lives, running the boarding house while Linc served as a deputy sheriff for the Western half of Sumner County. Linc told Florence about what he had done and they both would share a good laugh at Rawlind's expense. The banker never learned the secret of the hinged floorboard.

BRIGGS LOSES HIS HEART

■ MESSENGER OF DEATH

Chapter 1

D eath rode into Wolf Point, Thursday, on a lame horse. Looks can be deceiving, but there was no mistaking his intentions after that afternoon. He resembled hundreds of other range riders of that era. High crowned brown Stetson, jeans, checkered flannel shirt, Judson boots and a Colt .45 in a high-riding holster. None of the clothes were new and the knees of the jeans had been patched. He dismounted at the livery stable next to the blacksmith's forge.

"Howdy, mister," the blacksmith's son greeted him, *"yer horse pull up lame... er is it somethin' more serious?"*

Briggs handed the reins to the youngster, who appeared to be in his twelfth summer. He was thin, but strong looking and his hands showed the callous of hard labor. He was probably learning the blacksmith trade from his father. Briggs dusted off his clothes with his hat, before answering the lad.

"He got a rock stuck between his hoof an' the shoe. I couldn't work it loose with my knife an' I fear the shoe will have to come off. Can yuh get the blacksmith tuh take a look at it? I'm gonna be in town a while," Briggs explained.

"Yup, we uns will git him all fixed up fer yuh. Don't yuh worry none." the lad replied, leading the gelding toward the barn.

Briggs watched the limping horse and hoped there wasn't a permenant injury. The horse was a dusty roan color and shaggy looking, but he was a tough one who could run with the best and leave the grass fed Indian ponies in last place. He gazed up and down the main street. Hotel, drygoods store, general store, barber shop, the Silver Saddle saloon, a cooper shop, gunsmith, the Rolling Dollar Saloon, the blachsmith and livery barn, a sale barn for horses and cattle. The railroad station was off by itself. A stage line depot and the Wells Fargo office.

The bank appeared to be a sturdy building, weathered by the Dakota winters and baked by the summer sun. It, in all probability, had a sturdy vault to match. Well, no mind, he'd come here to kill a man, but knowing the lay of the town would help when the time came. The man he sought was a bounty hunter. In his estimation that was the lowest type of back shootin' snake in existance.

His younger brother Mason, had been buried a month ago. The young fellow had ridden into town to visit a girl he'd taken fancy to. Disappointment had met him a block from her house. He saw her walking to the Grange Hall dance with a dude in fancy clothes and they were laughing and talking like old friends. So Mason had hitched his horse in front of the Hardrock Saloon and entered the establishment with the intention of drowning his heartbreak and drown it he did.

Too much bar whiskey, consumed too quickly. Then he had been sick out back of the saloon, with the broken crates, empty bottles and weeds, he staggered out front. He bumped into the building and stumbled over some hidden trash.

He picked himself up from the ground wondering why on earth he'd been lying face down on the hard packed dirt. Mounting his horse had proved to be a difficult chore that took four tries. He rode out of town nearly falling from the saddle. As he rode the trail home, and was acting like a fool, singing and weaving in the saddle, he occasionally howled at the half-moon riding high overhead.

The bounty hunter, waiting in ambush for his victim, mistook Mason for his target. The lad was blown out of his saddle by a high impact, low velocity slug of 500 grains. His horse had found its way home with drying blood on the the saddle. Briggs and his brothers had searched the trail in the darkness, but it was nearly noon the following day they'd found his brush covered, half hidden, stone cold body.

Briggs had haunted the saloons and dives, in that part of Montana, for nearly a week before he'd heard a drunken whisper that told him who the ambusher had been. The trail had warmed as he had gotten closer. Overnighting on the trail, so as not to lose any time, and being caught in the cold rain, were not the most pleasant experiences he'd ever enjoyed, but Mason had been family and if the truth were known he and Briggs had been the closest of the brothers. He was relentless in his pursuit. The trail ended at Wolf Point and he hoped to face the man down before the week was done.

He walked to the Rolling Dollar saloon and gazed over the batwing doors until his eyes adjusted to the dim interior. Nobody in the saloon resembled the man he sought. Disappointed, he left to try the Longbranch saloon. Carmady, the backshooter he searched for had been described as a great bear of a man, hairy with a full beard, and standing over six feet tall. He was said to be fast with a six-gun, accurate with a rifle and a rough and tumble fighter of the first order. Some would say Briggs had taken on a tall order, hunting down the hunter, but he couldn't care less about others warnings. He knew his limitations and also his strong points.

As Briggs crossed the rutted street he paused to let a heavily laden, high wheeled freight wagon rumble by. The four mules were straining against the weight of the load and the mule skinner was turning the air blue with his cursing. He wasn't being stingy with his bull whip either and was cracking it again and again, over the backs of the straining beasts.

He stamped the dust off his boots on the boardwalk and ambled his way into the Longbranch saloon. He headed for the crowded bar, which was made of walnut and carved with fancy scrolls. The brass rails and the spitoons were polished to a gleaming gloss. It appeared someone cared about the appearence of of this place of business. Surely not the patrons who it seemed were busy gulping down their whiskey.

There appeared to be only one space left near the center of the bar. As Briggs squeezed in, he discovered someone had left a half full glass of whiskey setting on the bar. The fellows on each side of him turned his way and one of them spoke.

"I wouldn't take thet there spot iffin I was you, stranger," the man warned. *"Thets where Hamilton was drinkin' jest a moment ago and I'm shore he will be back presently."*

Briggs shrugged. *"Name don't make the earth shake fer me, mister."* he answered.

"No, bein' new here I don't spose yuh know his reputation. The bozo's never bin bested in a rough, an' tumble brawl." the man parted his hair. *"See this scar I got, an' these teeth I ain't?"* He grinned showing the gaps.

"Oh Lordy, mister here he comes back!" The man paled, and turned back to the bar. Briggs felt a heavy hand, on his shoulder, with a strong grip.

"I am gonna let yuh live, pilgrim, on a counta yer new here 'bouts, but yuh best be movin' outta my place. Thet's mah whiskey there in fronta yuh." The raspy voice warned.

Briggs turned to glance at the battle scarred veteran of a hundred brawls. He looked muscular, but slow. The man was at least in his late forties. Not much taller than his own five foot nine, but probably outweighed him by thirty pounds. Briggs turned back, and picked up the whiskey glass, turning it this way, and that, looking it over closely. He frowned.

"I'm losin' mah patience!" Hamilton grumbled.

"I don't see yer name on it." Briggs grinned, and downed the remaining whiskey. The bar-room became silent, as Briggs put the empty glass softly down on the bar. *"Hope I don't ketch hydro-phobia."*

He shrugged, wiping his mouth on the back of his hand. Then, with what was later described as lightning like speed, pivoted, and drove a lead right into the bigger man's solar plexus, with all the strength of his fist, arm, shoulder, back, and legs.

As the bruiser gasped for breath, Briggs grabbed his elbow, spun him around, slipped a full Nelson on him, smashed the man's face into the ornate bar, and threw him to the floor. Hamilton lay gasping, and bleeding, trying to gather enough strength to get up. He was surprised, not to say embarrassed, by the quick turn of events.

"Mister" he warned, *"when I git up offa the floor, I'm gonna*

encourage yuh tuh regret the day you was born, I'm gonna bust yuh up in so many pieces, yer jist gonna be dog meat, I'm gonna........" Briggs interrupted him:

"Are yuh gonna talk, er fight? yuh ain't showed me nothin' but yackity-yak 'bout what yuh say yer gonna do."

Briggs looked down at the gasping hardcase. As the man heaved himself upright, Briggs detected the furtive hand movement, as the bully scooped up a handful of sawdust from the floor. He faked a left jab, and threw the sawdust at Briggs' eyes. Briggs had expected it, and was ready. He leapt out of the way of the bigger man's charge, and smashed a wicked right into the area just below the ear. Hamilton crashed head-first into one of the support beams and the whole building shook. Briggs turned back to the bar.

"Bartender, the drinks are on Hamilton." he grinned... not breathing any harder.

He watched in the barback mirror as Hamilton staggered to his feet, and reached for his gun. It looked like Hamilton wasn't prepared to lose this fight and had decided to settle it his own way. Briggs turned, drew, and fired, putting a shot into Hamilton's chest before the man could pull the trigger. He holstered his Colt, and quoted from Briggs list of proverbs:

"When we're talkin' lightning, an' thunder, yuh always see the flash, for yuh hear the thunder. There lies Mister Thunder. May he rest in peace."

Most of the crowd was shocked into silence, but one man spoke what the others were probably thinking:

"I knew someday Hamilton would meet his match, but I expected the man who done it would be seven feet tall, and a yard wide." he seemed somewhat awed. *"Where did yuh learn tuh fight like thet?"* The crowd didn't seem impressed by the gunplay, but the whipping up on the bully, made them all sit up, and notice.

"From mah youngest sister, an' she kin still thump mah melon, three ways of Saturday. I come from uh big family, six broth-

ers, an' five sisters. Me? I'm now the runt of the litter, so I hadda learn early, er go hungry." Briggs explained. The town marshal appeared, and wanted to know what had happened. The talkative gent explained:

"Yuh know Hamilton, marshal, he was gittin' in this here pilgrim's face, like he's in uh habit of, but it seems this here gent eats Hamiltons fer breakfast. Whipped 'im far, an' square, which as yuh kin imagine, din't set well with are bully. He pulled iron, an' was gonna backshoot this man, but Hamilton din't git up early nuff this mornin'. Yuh kin see he's still uh sleepin'"

"Whipped him yuh say?" The marshal looked at Briggs with new respect, *"are yuh gonna be a new citizen of Wolf Point, er jist passin' through?"* Briggs shrugged.

"I ain't decided, as of yet, marshal, lookin' fer trouble ain't mah nature, but runnin' out on it ain't either. What I always say is: 'Iffin yer gonna prod the sleepy pup with uh stick, don't be surprised iffin he growls, an' bites yuh on the laig.'" Briggs quoted again from his list.

"Yuh can't be blamed fer defendin' yerself, so I ain't gonna file no charges, but watch yer back alla the time. There is some hardcases thet hit town ever so often, thet's plumb rattlesnake mean, an' don't care iffin ah man is facin', er walkin' away, if yuh git mah drift." the marshal warned as he turned, and left the saloon.

Briggs ordered a glass of bar whiskey, and sipped it slowly. This was not the way he wanted to slip unnoticed into town, but fate had a way of getting a strangle hold on the best laid plans of anyone, and he guessed this was one of those times. Well, maybe things would work out anyway.

He paid his tab, and left the saloon. Walking the side streets, and searching for a rooming house was a lost cause. There were none to be had. It was a pleasant, well laid out town he noticed as he tipped his hat to the few ladies he met on his trek. Well, it was going to have to be the hotel, or the hay mow of the livery barn. He decided on the hotel, and made his way back to the main street of Wolf Point.

It wasn't much, as hotels go. The weathered raw wood on the outside reminded Briggs of nearly all the business buildings in this part of the West. Whitewash was fine for fences, and barns, but letting Mother nature do it, was easier, and more permanent. The lobby wasn't any better. A shabby, threadbare, gloomy, down, and out place to do business. The clerk was surly, or indifferent depending on which ever mood struck him at the moment. He was reading a Ned Buntline dime novel, and didn't really want to be bothered. He was so engrossed in the story, he didn't look up until Briggs slammed his saddlebags down on the counter.

"Mister, iffin yuh kin drag yerself away from yer education, fer I moment, I'd sign the register," he told the indifferent clerk.

The man looked really put upon, as he laid his novel face down on the counter, so he wouldn't lose his place, and pushed the register toward the front of the counter. He held a pen out at the same time. Briggs took the proffered pen, and signed, 'Briggs Clayborn' in neat script, then shoved the register back at the clerk.

"Room 23, upstairs front, two bits."

The man was already involved in 'head em off at the pass', and licked his thumb, as he turned another page. Briggs dropped two dimes, and a nickel on the counter. The busy clerk reached with one hand, and pushed the coins into a cigar box, without looking up, or missing a word.

The staircase was narrow, and steep, but with nothing bulky to carry, the climb wasn't much of a chore. Down the hall he found his room, and opened the door, which had a broken lock. He was somewhat surprised at the condition of the room. It was timeworn, but the bedding was clean, and there didn't appear to be any roaches to share the nightstand with. The lamp chimney was clear of any smoke smudges. A faded floral pattern wallpaper, of a non-descript color covered the walls, and most likely hid a multitude of mistakes, and accidents. It had pulled loose near the corner where two walls met, and he could see a widening crack in the plaster. The feedmill calendar, tacked to the wall, read 'June 1897.' This was the last day of the month, and the hot summer was about to settle in. It had been an early, wet spring, and the countryside had burst into green all at once, it seemed. Briggs' thoughts were interrupted by the sound of a closed fist meeting flesh. The meaty smack of it was familiar to him, but the soft sobbing that grew more insistent, after what sounded like open handed slaps, upset his sense of tranquility. He'd have to investigate. He knocked on the door of room 25 and the sobs became more pronounced.

"Is everthin' awright in there? Does anyone need any help?" he called.

Heavy footsteps advanced toward the closed door. The knob turned and the door swung open. A very hefty, red haired woman, taller than average, and weighing near three hundred pounds, but with an angelic face, answered him in a husky voice.

"No problem here, Mister, jist me an' mah man havin' uh family feud."

She jerked her thumb over her shoulder at the quivering geezer who stood by a chair. Blood dripped from his nose, and one eye was nearly swollen shut. She outweighed him by nearly one hundred eighty pounds.

"The little weasels' been holdin' out on me. He won over twelve bucks uh playin' poker, an' was gonna keep it all fer hisself, but I persuaded him tuh turn it over tuh me fer some of the finer things of life, like staples, yuh know flour, bacon, lard, sugar, an' uh bottle uh rotgut. I think the bandy legged little twerp has learned his lesson fer now, but sooner er later he's gonna try this stunt, er some other one, an' I'll have to smack him silly again. Yuh know pokin' yer nose inta other folks business kin buy yuh more grief than yuh kin handle." The lady explained.

"Far be it from me tuh interfere in uh fambly affair, ma'am, I was uh hopin' tuh prevent mayhem, an' act as uh peacemaker, but I kin see yuh got the situation well in hand, so tuh speak, so I'll bid yuh uh 'good evenin' an' be on mah way." Briggs left the heavyweight standing in her doorway, and returned to his room, muttering low: *"When in the camp of the Romans, it's best tuh speak Latin without uh drawl."* another of his proverbs.

Briggs sat on his bed and rolled himself a smoke. The bag of tobacco was nearly empty and it was his last one. He had enough papers to last another week, and wondered why he never ran out of both at the same time. A trip to the general store was a must, to replenish his supply. As he smoked, he thought about the skinny pup of a man in the next room and was reminded, *'love is blind.'* After thinking on that for a time, he came to the conclusion that, in this case, love was also deaf and dumb. Especially dumb, but who was he to judge without walking a mile in the other man's shoes?

The stub of his cigarette burned his fingers, and caused him to drop it on the floor. He arose, and ground it into the carpet with his bootheel. He raised the chimney, and lit the hanging lamp, turned down the wick, and lowered the chimney back into place. Hunger was beginning to gnaw on his innards like a mouse, and he would have to find a place to slip on the feedbag. How to find a place to in a small town usually wasn't any problem. Just ask anybody. Anybody except the busy room clerk. He left the lamp burning in his room, and tromped down the staircase. The clerk was still living in the adventure of his dime novel, and didn't see Briggs leave.

Carmady Turns Up
Chapter 2

Carmady had been bunking with a rough, and tough bunch of cut throats, who were loosely banded together, not in what you'd call a gang, but they shared meals, experiences, and comradeship with others in the outlaw fringe. If a horse pulled up lame, another could be borrowed without a hassle.

A line shack up in the foothills, out of the way of traveled trails, was called home for the present. The county sheriff either hadn't discovered it, or had chosen not to, for reasons of his own. Carmady was of the opinion the latter was the case, as not much in the way of law breaking ever escaped any lawmans' notice for very long.

A half dozen of the bunch sat around the dying campfire drinking coffee, and swapping lies. The evening fare had been the usual beans, and bacon, which had drawn some complaints. Carmady had half a notion to scout around the surrounding country, and find a yearling cow to butcher, but couldn't get anyone to go along with the idea. The taste of fresh meat was what he missed the most, and as he dumped the last dregs, and drops out of his cup, he decided to saddle up, and head for the nearest town.

He had some money to spend, and poker, women, and booze were on his list of things to do, but not necessarily in that order. Maybe even a rough, and tumble brawl with a town rowdy would satisfy the itch he hadn't been able to scratch, since he'd been on the dodge.

Hell, it hadn't been his fault. In the dark all cats are gray, and he'd been half asleep when the horse had come lopin' around the bend in the trail. Without hesitation he'd blown the cowboy out of his saddle, and then to his dismay, discovered the man he killed was just a boy. He had lit out the same night, looking over his shoulder for the first few miles. He'd been lucky and hoped his luck would hold.

He put his cup away and heaved his saddle off the corral fence.

"Where yuh headed, Carmady?" Old Bascome wondered.

"Got a itch I can't scratch, an' I'm gonna mosey inta town, an' see a man 'bout a horse, er his daughter 'bout a itch." Carmady grinned.

"Don't be a gallopin' back here howlin' at the moon, all the

way, an' showin' some posse where we live." Bascome warned. Carmady just looked at the old bum with disgust.

"Whacha take me fer a greenhorn? Yuh shouldn't even hafta say thet!" he scowled, *"yuh want I should bring yuh a bottle uh red eye fer tuh keep yuh warm?"* Carmady asked.

The oldtimer's eyes lit up like it was Christmas. *"Durn betcha, Carmady, I cud kiss yuh fer a bottle uh pop skull."*

"Yuh do I'll bust it over yer head, yuh ole fool." Carmady laughed, and led his horse out of the corral.

He mounted and debated on which direction to take. Wolf Point was closer, and easier to get to, and the Silver Saddle saloon stayed open all night, but their prices were higher. What the hell. It was only money. He turned his horse toward Wolf Point, and coaxed him to a trot.

Carmady loped into the south edge of town an hour, and a half later, and headed right for the Silver Saddle. He'd heard, by way of gossip, there was a bozo that hung around there who would maybe give him a little rough, an' tumble action. Went by the name of Hamilton, and twas said he'd never been bested, as yet. Yah! the town champs, they were his kind of fighters. He really needed a good workout. He tied his horse at the hitchrack out front, and stepped up into the lit up, noisy interior.

The bar was busy, and half a dozen saloon girls were circulating around the room trying to drum up more business.

"Well don't fear, Carmady's here!" he bellered, but wasn't heard over the uproar.

He didn't have any trouble finding a spot at the counter near the back door. The bartender spotted him and without asking, put a glass in front of him, and began to pour. When the glass was half full the bartender was ready to stop, but Carmady held one large forefinger on the neck of the bottle until the glass was brim full. He winked at the barkeep, and dropped a silver dollar on the polished wood. The barkeep shrugged, and left him a half dollar, and a quarter in it's place.

Carmady tipped his head back, and downed half the glass in three gulps. He put his glass on the bar, and turned to survey the room. There were poker games at the deal tables. The piano plunker was lazily banging away on the ivory keys.

Near the center of the room a cowboy was dancing with one of the painted ladies, and doing a poor job of it. He had his bottle in one hand, and was tasting it occasionally. His eyes were becoming glassy, and he was staring into space, unfocused.

Carmady didn't see anyone who would give him much of a battle. He turned back to the bar, and motioned to the barkeep. The man brought the bottle back and refilled Carmady's glass.

"Where's Hamilton tonight?" He asked.

The barkeep looked at him strangely. *"Yuh a friend uh his?"* he paused to wipe at the bartop with a rag.

"Nope, I wuz hopin' fer uh little rough, an' tumble. Actually I ain't never met the man, but heard uh his rep." Carmady took another swig of whiskey.

"Well, yuh ain't heard the news then. Earlier this afternoon, he more er less tangled with uh wildcat, an' thet there gent bounced him off the bar uh couple uh times, an' then mopped up the floor with what was left uh him. Hamilton weren't prepared tuh lose the fight, so he pulled iron whilst this here gent's back was turned, but he was way too slow, an' the pilgrim give him uh permanent case uh lead poisinin'" The barkeep explained.

Carmady received this news with disappointment. After getting all primed up for some entertainment, now the damn fool had got hisself killed.

"How 'bout this bruiser that done him in. He here 'bouts?" Carmady wondered hopefully.

The barman smiled, showing crooked teeth. *"The bruiser, yuh speak of, is probley checked inta the hotel, or out an' 'bout I lookin' fer some supper 'bout now, but iffin yuh go lookin' fer him, don't set yer sights too high. The pilgrim ain't but five foot nine, an' 'bout one sixty five in weight, but don't git fooled like Hamilton was. Thet pilrgim is pure fight, an' uh yard wide."*

There wasn't much to gain, or a lot of fun thumping a smaller man. Usually the crowd became hostile when a feller totaled one, and it was somewhat of a no win situation. He sipped some more of his whiskey, and wondered why he was so disappointed. His dour mood didn't last very long.

He looked up in time to see a buckskin clad mountain man stroll through the batwings, carrying a Sharps buffalo blaster. This bozo was his size, or may have out weighed him a bit. He knew from experience the mountain folks were always spoiling for a good rough, an' tumble, no holds barred, kick, gouge, bite, choke, and smash, fun filled fight.

"YEEEEEE...HAAAAAAA!!!" Carmady bellered, *"come up tuh the bar, an' lemme buy yuh a drink 'fore I beat yer brains out, mountain man!"*

It must have been music to the stranger's ears, as he broke out in a grand gap-toothed grin, and headed right for Carmady. *"Don't mind iffin I do, pardner, an' here I thunk it was gonna be a dull night. Ut's so hard tuh find somebody big 'nuff fer uh good rough, an' tumble. Grover's mah name, an' whiskey's mah drink, so set 'em up, mah new friend, an' then we 'uns ull have at it!"* the mountain tracker was delighted.

Carmady and Grover sized each other up as they worked their way through their whiskey. The bartender was dubious, and warned them that any damage would have to be paid for, which was standard.

The mountain man handed his Sharps to the bartender, who stood it in a corner behind the bar, and the two heavyweights squared off.

Carmady circled to his right, and feinted a left jab. Grover didn't fall for the jab. He kicked Carmady in the knee, and dropped him with a heavy right to the ribs. The punch hurt, but it wasn't anything he'd never felt before.

He bounced up and charged, catching Grover by surprise. As he backpedaled, his legs tangled with a chair. He rolled, and jumped up grabbing a chair which he used to smash Carmady over the head.

Carmady saw stars, and felt the blood running down the side of his face. He pawed at it to clear his eyes, and circled right again. He delivered a surprise kick to Grover's belly, and received a solid blow to the kidney. He shot two jabs, and threw a heavy right uppercut that caught Grover coming in. He rolled his eyes back, and his knees began to buckle, but he shook his head to clear it, and bored in again. His next punch caught Carmady flush on the jaw. The big man nearly lost his balance. He grabbed the bar edge, with one beefy hand, and saved himself from a fall to the floor.

The mountain man jumped in to finish him off, but Carmady was ready for the assault. He lashed out with his boot, and tripped Grover. As the man was falling, Carmady locked his fists together, and brought them down together on the other man's neck, and bringing his knee up at the same time catching him in the face. Grover fell unconscious to the floor. The fight was over, and Carmady was secretly glad. It had been a great way to blow off steam, and get rid of tensions, but he wasn't in as good a shape as he'd like to be.

It was five minutes before Grover stirred, and sat up with a groan. Carmady held out his hand, and helped him up.

"Good fight, coulda gone yer way jist as easy, mountain man, les have 'nother drink." he clapped Grover on the back.

"Yuh whupped me far, 'an square, Mister, an' I don't even know yer name." Grover grinned.

The winner laughed, and asked the bartender to leave the bottle. *"Call me Carmady, mah friend, an' les finish off this here whiskey."*

They stood at the bar, and swilled down what was left of the bottle. Afterward Grover collected his Sharps from the bartender and they left together to find some supper.

Fair Warning

Chapter 3

Briggs walked to the Hungry Horse Cafe and hoped the food was better than the name they'd picked. The place was crowded, and if that was any indication, maybe the food was okay.

He found a table against the wall a girl was just wiping off, and headed in that direction. He studied the menu that was printed in chalk on a slate fastened to the wall.

When he turned back there were two large men standing there. They both looked as if they'd been through the Civil War again. One had a crude bandage wrapped around his head and the other's eye was nearly swelled shut. Both of their lips looked swollen.

"Mister, would yuh mind, too much, iffin we shared yer table, seein' the place is mighty busy?" The bruiser with the head bandage asked.

Briggs shrugged, and pointed to the remaining chairs. *"Set, gents, an' put on the feedbag. You fellers been stuffin' wildcats inta gunny sacks, er whot?"* he grinned.

The buckskin clad man snorted, and laughed out loud. *"Does 'pear thet way don't it? But tuh answer yer question, we jest had us a friendly rough, an' tumble over at the saloon. This bozo jist whupped me, which I might mention, ain't been did too often."*

Briggs reached into his shirt pocket, and took out his sack of tobacco, and papers. He rolled himself a smoke, as he studied the two men, and then tossed the makin's onto the table in front of the two, as a friendly gesture.

"Yuh must be a mountain man come tuh town fer tuh blow off some steam, an' you, I venture, hunt fer a livin' be it men, er animals." Briggs blew a puff of smoke ceilingward.

The mountain man picked up the papers, and tobacco. The other geezer looked at him strangely.

"Yore very preceptive, cowboy, how did yuh know?"

Briggs didn't answer right away, but seemed to study the glowing end of his cigarette.

"Yer name would be Carmady, iffin I'm not mistaken, an' I been tryin' tuh ketch up with yuh fer quite uh spell. Yer friend, here I don't know of, but you I've come tuh kill. Be it guns, knives, er beat yuh tuh death don't make no nevermind."

Carmady shifted in his chair, and looked uncomfortable. *"No matter whot yuh think, Mister, it was a accident, an' iffin yer a relitave uh his'n, I am truly sorry."* He sounded sincere.

"Makes no difference, Carmady, a man should always make sure uh his target, an' thet would eliminate any chance uh gunnin' down a sixteen year old, unarmed boy. Everbody is entitled tuh his own opinion, an' mine is thus: Huntin' down men fer the money on their heads is a low down coward's way way uh livin', but shootin' from ambush is even worse." Briggs stated.

Grover squinted at Carmady, out of the one eye that wasn't closed. He stood, and picked up his Sharps rifle.

"I had no idee. This runs again the grain uh the mountain man's code uh conduct. Carmady, yuh whupped me far, an' square, an' thet I do respect yuh fer, but a money shooter thet hunts down a man fer the reward on his head, I cain't call a friend, so weuns er partin' company as uf now." Grover nodded to Briggs, and left the cafe.

"Little man, yuh've tookin' on a tall order iffin yuh think I'm jist gonna roll over an' die cause yuh say so. Kill me iffin yuh kin, but I don't think yer man enough, **iffin** *were talkin' rough, an' tumble, no holds barred. Since yuh've challenged me, I'm gonna name the time, an' place. Sattaday mornin' out behind the saloon, no guns. This is gonna give yuh a couple uh nights tuh sleep on it, an' think 'bout it. Iffin yuh change yer mind, jist leave town quiet like an' it'll all be forgot."* Carmady said. *"Now iffin yuh don't mind I'm gonna have mah supper, as yuh knew who I was when yuh invited me tuh set."*

The harried waitress arrived to take their orders. Briggs ordered beefsteak, fried taters, apple pie, and coffee. Carmady wanted pork chops, smashed taters, gravy, and green beans. The men ate their supper in silence, and left the cafe. Each with their own thoughts.

Briggs had come to the end of a long trail and found the man he meant to kill. He knew Carmady would do his best to do him in, and if the bigger man was successful, so be it. He'd noticed Carmady had stated 'no guns', but hadn't made mention of any other weapons, so he wouldn't be much surprised at anything the man came up with, as he knew his life was at stake.

Briggs returned to the hotel, and climbed the stairs to his room. He couldn't help but think about Saturday, and wonder what kind of a sneaky trick Carmady would come up with. He knew people didn't change, and it was a man hunters' nature to have the edge no matter what the situation.

He undressed slowly, staring at the door, and wishing he had a chair to brace under the knob. He was in a habit of sleeping in his longjohns with his Colt under the pillow, and wasn't about to change his ways.

He blew out the lamp, and felt his way to the bed. Briefly he wondered if his horse had come out of his stone injury without any permanent lameness, and decided to check on him in the morning. He rolled over on his side, and drifted off to sleep.

His sleep was interrupted later, by a trio of cowboys singing offkey, and shooting holes in the moon with their six-guns. He had no trouble falling asleep again.

Later, when two mounted horses galloped up the street outside, Briggs turned over to his other side, and mumbled in his sleep. Shortly after that, the furtive sound of the doorknob turning was enough to bring him back from his light sleep. He gripped his six shooter and slid it out from under his pillow. The shadowy figure that slipped through the doorway was not near big enough to be Carmady, but the underhanded bozo could have hired someone to do his dirty work. The figure approached the stand where he'd left his clothes, then bent over to flip open the cover of his saddlebags he'd left on the floor.

Briggs tensed, and leapt out of bed, bringing the Colt down across the man's head with authority. Without a gasp, or groan, the sneak fell to the floor, like a bag of dirty laundry, unconscious. Briggs lit a match, and raised the chimney of the lamp to light it. He peered down to see who, or what he'd pistol whipped. It was the narrow-faced mouse from room 25.

No doubt he, and his ton-of-fun mate, supplemented their meager income in this manner. The little man was shoeless, and dressed in black. He, more than likely, slipped in, and out of the hotels' rooms occupied by heavy sleepers, with ease. Briggs had half a notion to toss the little sneak thief out the window, but it probably wouldn't do more than cripple him up. So Briggs just sat on his bed, and waited for him to come around.

A moth, attracted by the glowing lamplight, insanely crashed into the hot chimney again, and again. Each time knocking dust from it's wings, and body. It was a single minded attack Briggs knew the insect could never win.

The man stirred, and with a pitiful groan, began to rub the spot on his head where Briggs had tried his best to bend the barrel of his Colt six-gun. Finally he sat up and stared at Briggs.

"Sorry, Mister, but you have no idea what kind of a life I lead. She keeps me on such short rations, I never have any spending money and you know yourself there are things a man needs." He continued to rub his sore skull.

"An' yuh can't leave her because yuh love her, right? I know love has put together some strange unions an' yuh can't duck Dan Cupid's arras when he flings em." Briggs grinned.

"All of that and she depends on me. She's helpless without me." The man stated.

"Helpless? Hah! she's 'bout helpless as a she bear with cubs, er a bull what sees red." Briggs snorted.

"Not helpless about physical things, no not at all, but its that she can't read, or write. About money though, she don't let one red cent slip through her fingers. Matter of fact she squeezes each coin until the Indian on the face of it lets out a war whoop." The man replied.

Briggs stared at the man intently for more than a minute. Finally the sneak thief couldn't meet Briggs angry stare, and looked down at the floor, waiting for the worst.

"Listen, yuh spineless little varment, I don't keer whot yuh do out, an' 'bout the hotel fer the rest uh the night, but iffin I ketch yuh uh playin' sticky fingered Joe in mah room again, I ain't gonna be Mister Nice Guy no more. Had uh notion tuh heave yuh outa the winder in the furst place." Briggs warned.

The smaller man looked up with relief, and heaved himself to his feet. He nodded, and scurried out of the room like the mouse he resembled. It felt like dawn be could approaching, and when he checked the hands on the dial of his stemwinder, it was confirmed. Four forty five.

Briggs blew the lamp out, and lay on the bed again, watching the sky lighten, as the sun began to rise above the horizon. Robins were beginning to chirp, and the crickets were becoming silent. Briefly he wished he'd had a proverb to leave the mousey sneak thief with, but his list didn't cover this occasion. Maybe something like *'When you draw short straw, and get sent out for the cheese, make sure the cat has been put out for the night'* Aw nuts! he'd have to work on it.

He felt across the nightstand for his tobacco, and papers. The sack only had enough crumbs of Bull Durham to roll a skinny cigarette, and it would have to be enough to satisfy his nicotine urge. He lit up, and let the smoke leak out of his nose. Today he'd have to get a new sack, or two of tobacco. Sleep was out of the question now, and what Carmady had said about sleeping on what he was to face on Saturday morning, was beginning to worry at him in spite of his attitude about fate. What the Hell, nobody really wants to die.

He sat on the edge of the bed, and tried to think of something he could do to ruffle Carmady's feathers, and put him on edge.

The Widows' Ordeal
Chapter 4

It was an arduous task being a single woman, and trying to compete in a man's world. Men, it appeared, had countless opportunities, and manners in which to support themselves, but a womans' province was limited. There were many jobs she knew she could manage, but would never be given the chance to prove.

The second tribulation was her twelve year old daughter. No man, or at least none she had met, wanted the responsibility of raising a youngster. Well, that wasn't exactly true. There had been Morton, and his hard scrabble farm. Backbreaking labor from dawn to dusk, for the both of them was not the childhood she would have chosen for little Carrie. She had never been a healthy, husky baby. Carrie hadn't been able to gain the weight she needed, and was even now thin, and fragile.

Helping out, in Polk's General store, on Monday, Wednesday, and Friday afternoons, and working mornings six days a week, plus all day Tuesday, Thursday, and Saturday, at Hall's Dining hall, allowed them to eke out a meager existence, but didn't allow her much time with Carrie. The girl was reaching the age where she really needed her mother, and she was, of course, asking questions that Laura tried to answer honestly at a twelve year old level Carrie could understand.

Laura's husband had left them on their own, while he had tried his luck in the gold fields of the Yukon, but having heard no word from him in more than two, and a half years, Laura believed he had met an untimely undoing. She had heard the stories about the claim jumpers, and leeches that waited until someone had struck color, and then relieved them of their gold, and life at the same time.

It was Thursday evening, and the dining hall had been particularly busy, and crowded, but it seemed everyone had finished their meals, and had gone on their way quickly. Their conversations had centered mainly on the fight at the Silver Saddle saloon, and the death of one roughneck by the name of Hamilton. The name was familiar to her, as the man had once roughed her up.

The memory of that evening was still fresh, and painful. It had been a Saturday night nearly three weeks ago she had been about ready to hang out at the Silver Saddle saloon, just to satisfy a biological urge she had kept suppressed. What she wanted was a commitment. She thought about this as she neared the little house where she and Carrie lived.

Carrie had the table set, and a fire in the cookstove. She was a sweet daughter, and did these things on her own with no complaints. Laura noticed though, the girl kept her eyes downcast, and was unusually quiet.

"Carrie, what is it?, I can tell something is wrong, was anyone here today?" Laura asked.

Carrie glanced up briefly. *"No, nobody was here."* The girl answered, as she traced a pattern on the floor with her shoe toe.

"What is it Carrie, you know we can talk about anything."

Carrie paused, and looked up at her mother. She seemed to be shy, and embarrassed about it, whatever it was. She stared at the floor again.

"Mother, today...I..I became a woman." Carrie stammered.

A shock ran through Laura. Not little Carrie! How? When? she'd said there had been no one here today. If it was that Adams boy...

"Carrie, tell me, what are we talking about?"

"We talked about it before, mother, remember when you told me about monthlies? I got my first one today, and it scared me until I remembered the talk we had, and how it's a natural thing that happens to most all ladies early in their life." Carrie replied.

The relief was so great, Laura let out the breath she didn't realize she'd been holding, and here she had thought that Carrie had.., but she should have known better. Carrie would never.., but then in the heat of passion, who knows what might happen?

She hugged her daughter, and asked, *"What shall we have for supper, dear?"*

Carrie told her she had peeled potatoes, carrots, and onions, how about stew?

AN EDGE?

Chapter 5

Briggs sat on the edge of the bed, and stared out the window at the awakening town. Across the street a merchant with sleeves rolled up, swept the boardwalk in front of his store, raising a small cloud of dust. Even though the store front was in the shade of the early morning sun, he was sweating, and the back of his clean white shirt was sticking to him. It was going to be a dog day, for sure.

He stood, stripped off his longjohns, and poured water into the wash basin. The sliver of soap he found on the stand was less than he had hoped for, but it would have to do the job.

Briggs, thought about the upcoming meeting with the back-shooting man hunter, and weighing his chances. The man was a brute, and outweighed him by nearly forty pounds. He would have to rely on speed and surprise. If the man managed to wrap his long arms around him, pinning his arms to his sides, his chances of winning, or even surviving would be extremely doubtful. That would be something he must avoid at all cost.

He rinsed, and dried, and then soaped his face. He reached for his razor, and began to scrape the nights growth of whiskers. Soon the shaving was done, and he rinsed off the remaining soapy lather. As he was folding his razor, a thought entered his mind. His experience with rough and tumble fights had taught him to expect the unexpected, and sure as Monday followed the Sabbath, whats-his-face, would in all probability, if the fight was not going to his liking, whip out a skinning knife and try to pare him down to the bones.

His razor, although no match for the heavy knife, could, if wielded in the proper manner, be the salvation he needed. He slipped the folded razor into his left boot, and this was another thing the other man didn't know about him. Although he had taught himself, through hours and hours of practice, to draw and fire his Colt with his right hand, he was indeed a southpaw by birth. He finished his dressing with clean longjohns and shirt. Then as he stepped down the hotel stairs, he wondered if there was indeed another place to find breakfast. The day man had replaced the surly clerk of yesterday, so Briggs asked him about a morning meal.

"Why yes, there's Hall's Dining Hall on one of the side

streets. Just go two blocks East, and turn right. It's in the middle of the block on the left hand side. You can't miss it."

As he stepped out the lobby entrance door he spotted Carmady, his hands cupped, lighting a cigarette as he walked toward him. Briggs stepped back out of sight. As Carmady came even with the entrance, Briggs jumped out, drew his Colt, and pointed it right between the man's eyes.

"Yuh coulda been uh dead man, Carmady, but not now. Maybe later today, er maybe tomarra. Ya'll never know whin it's a commin'. Now yuh got sumpthin' tuh gnaw on yer mind. Try not tuh lose any sleep, yuh hear?"

Briggs grinned into the startled man's face and holstered his six gun. Without a doubt he had given Carmady a start, and hopefully it would work in his favor. He walked on down the street, and as he turned the corner, he looked back. Carmady was still standing in the same spot, scowling. Good enough.

He found Hall's without any trouble, and entered. It was about half full of patrons, most of whom were attacking their first meal of the day with gusto. He sat at one of the oilcloth covered tables, and waited for one of the serving girls to find him. The lady that came to his table was older. Probably in her late twenties, not homley but more on the order of good looking and neatly dressed. Her dark brown hair falling in long tresses.

Her eyes were the most striking feature of her make up. They were colored a pale, almost white-blue. Something about the lady, that Briggs could not understand immediately, struck his fancy, and he was attracted to her in a manner he hadn't felt since school days and his first puppy love.

"Good morning, sir, and what will you have for breakfast?" she smiled and Briggs fell in love.

"Top uh mornin' to yuh Miss, Ah'll have strangled aggs, side meat, an' fried taters, an' don't fergit the coffee." Briggs grinned like an idiot at her. He couldn't help himself. This woman seemed to bring out the humor in him.

She smiled back, and blushed. *"It's not miss, I'm a widow*

with a twelve year old daughter. Are you the man who done in Hamilton yesterday? If you are I want to thank you kindly, and shake your hand. For personal reasons, God forgive me, I'm glad he's dead."

Briggs stood, and took her hand in both of his, looking into those pale blue eyes: *"Ma'am ut's never a pleasure tuh kill a man, but iffin he done yuh some harm, then tis all tuh the well, an' good, the man was a bully, an' a braggart. Iffin it hadn't been me it woulda been someone else, sooner er later."*

"I better get your order in so's you can eat." Laura blushed again, and retreived her hand.

"Come on back tuh mah table later, ma'am I purely delight in talkin' to yuh, an' glory in the sound uh yer voice, reminds me uh one uh them there wind chimes I heerd once in Kansas City."

The lady hurried back to the kitchen. Briggs reached for his tobacco, before he remembered it was all gone. Lordy!, but a cigarette would taste good about now, and even better after a meal. He looked around the dining hall, to see if he could spot a familiar face. The mountain man that Carmady had whipped yesterday was sullenly putting away his breakfast. Briggs stood and walked over to where Grover sat.

"Mountain man, cud I mebee, barra 'nuff tobacco tuh make me a cigarette?" Grover looked up and his face took on an embarrassed look.

"I don't wancha tuh ever git the idee I was friends with thet there backshooter, soons I found out I cut out. Yuh kin unnerstan' me not knowin' whot kind o' lowlife he was."

"I know how mountain folks live, an' I ain't blamin' yuh one bit, so stand easy." Briggs replied.

"Listen iffin yuh gonna rough, n' tumble with thet snake, yuh wanna watch out fer the sneaky pup, but there's one thing I did learn. He don't see to good outa his left eye, an' he's easy tuh hit in the ribs on thet side, er mahap a neck shot." Grover tossed him a worn tobacco sack.

Briggs took out paper, and rolled himself a cigarette.

"I do thank yuh fer the tip, an' I'll shore keep thet in mind. Thanks fer the tobacco, friend."

He strolled back to his own table. He had the cigarette half smoked when the lady returned with his meal. How, he wondered, do these girls keep all those plates, and cups balanced on their arms clear from the kitchen? She smiled as she placed Briggs breakfast on his table.

"I don't really have the time to talk with you, as this is a busy time, but I get off at noon, and it would be a pleasure to have you walk me home then, Mister Briggs."

Briggs stared into those light blue eyes, and knew there was no way he could refuse, come Hell, high water, or Carmady.

"Ah'd be proud tuh Miss........er......."

"Oh I'm sorry, it's Laura Stevens, please call me Laura." she corrected.

"Laura," he spoke her name, *"name means noble, er royal, what a purty name, an' it really fits yuh, yuh know?"* How he loved talking to this woman! Now he had a double reason for disposing of Carmady in jig time.

Laura said, *"Later, Mr. Briggs, I must get back to my serving."* and she blessed him with a dazzling smile.

Briggs slowly devoured his breakfast, enjoying the taste of it. As he was downing the last swallow of coffee, he had the feeling of being watched. It was Carmady, just inside the entrance door. He wondered how long the man had been standing there and had he seen the exchange between Laura, and himself? Carmady just stood with massive hands on hips, stared at Briggs for what seemed a full minute, and then turned, and left the dining hall.

The expression on his face had been consternation, as though he'd been trying to figure out the smaller man's plans. Briggs shrugged it off, and left a half dollar on the table, as he stood, and left the dining hall. He planned to walk over to the livery stable to check on his horse. As he glanced back over his shoulder, he discovered Laura was watching him with a demure expression.

Briggs left the dining hall, and walked over to the livery stable. The morning sun was making it's presence known, as there wasn't a cloud in sight. Although he tried to stay in the shade of the buildings, and the few trees that lined the streets, he was sweating quite profusely by the time he'd reached his destination.

He stepped into the slightly cooler interior of the livery barn, and took off his Stetson. He wiped his forehead on the sleeve of his shirt, and sighed.

"'nother scorcher, huh?" A voice floated out from the gloomy interior.

"Thet it tis." Briggs replied, *"Wonderin' how mah horse is farin'? He's the shaggy roan gelding thet had uh rock in his hoof?"*

"Iffin yuh kin keep from ridin' him fer a couple uh days, I believe he'll recover without a limp, an' be goods new by Monday." The hostler replied. Briggs noticed the man wasn't as brawny as black-smiths usually were, but was tall, and lean with powerful looking arms, and shoulders.

"Got 'im in the third stall there iffin yuh wanta take a look at 'im." The man advised.

"Big Red," Briggs called, and heard the horse nicker at the sound of his voice. He stepped over to the stall, and petted the horse on the nose, and neck. The horse seemed glad to see him, and he wished he'd thought to bring an apple, or lump of sugar for a treat. As he petted the horse he was thinking about Carmady, and how he could find a way to shake up the man again. If there was a way he could find where he was without Carmady seeing him, and get in his face again, it would definitely grate on his composure. As his eyes wandered about the interior of the barn, he spotted the ladder to the haymow. Inspiration being the mother of invention, an idea came to him. He asked the hostler if he'd mind if he watched the street from the haymow for a few minutes.

"Not uh tall, mah friend, jist don't be smokin', up there, an'

126

light mah barn afire." The hostler answered.

Briggs climbed the ladder and made his way to the closed double doors at the front of the haymow. He watched the activity on the street through the space between the doors.

Freight wagons, men on horses, a carriage or two, people walking about. A black, and white non descript, mutt of a dog waited, and then dodged between a team of slow moving horses, and the wagon they were pulling. The mountain man he'd borrowed a bait of tobacco from, mounted his horse, and headed west, toward the far-away peaks. There was a small boy rolling a barrel hoop down the dusty street with a short stick. He was running to keep up, and doing a good job of keeping the hoop in motion.

Carmady stepped from the doorway of the general store, and appeared to be carefully looking over his surroundings, and scanning up, and down the street. Briggs grinned, and wondered if he had indeed put the man on edge.

As he watched, Carmady wandered up the street, and entered the Longbranch saloon. Satisfied Briggs stepped over to the ladder, and carefully made his way down to the barn floor again.

"Much 'bliged." Briggs tipped his hat to the hostler and left the barn. He took a round about way to get to the saloon, and approached the rear of the building, through the weeds, and broken glass, empty tin cans, and trash. He tried the rear door, and was relieved to find it unlocked. It squealed in protest as he carefully pushed it open, but the noise inside the saloon covered the sound.

This was a storeroom, and contained barrels of beer, and whiskey, a three legged table aslant near the wall, and a few broken chairs. As Briggs stood in the gloom, and stared out into the saloon, he found Carmady with foot on rail sipping at a glass of whiskey, and watching one of the barmaids do an impromptu jig on the dance floor, all by herself.

The man's back was to him, as he slipped out of the storage room, and up behind the bigger man. Briggs reached out, and pulled the man's six-gun from it's holster, cocked the hammer, and confronted the startled Carmady as the man whirled to face him.

"Aw, 'twould be a shame tuh kill a man with his own gun, now wouldn't it?" Briggs stared the man in the face, *"but today's not yer day, Carmady."*

He spoke quietly, as he eased the hammer back down, reversed the gun, and handed it back to the shaken man. *"Sleep well."*

He grinned as he walked out of the saloon. He had definiatley shaken the man up, and soon he'd be jumping at loud noises and shadows.

Briggs headed to the general store and when he was inside, he inhaled the odors of leather, new cloth, moth cakes, cakes of soap, and cured animal pelts. He stepped up to the counter, and asked the clerk for some cigarette papers, and a couple sacks of Bull Durham. He also wanted a box of wooden matches, a handful of beef jerky, and a slice of cheese. He dropped a quarter on the counter and was surprised when the clerk returned it to him.

"I wanna thank yuh fer doin' in thet bully Hamilton, as he has thumped me fer no reason on occasion, an' I fer one em glad he's dead."

Briggs returned the quarter. *"Sorry mah friend, I don't kill fer money. Be it twenty-five cents er five hunnerd dollars. Thet's mah rules I live by, an' I ain't gonna compromise."*

"Then would yuh accept a gift, as one friend tuh 'nother?" The clerk wondered.

Briggs pondered a moment. *"No, sorry, it 'mounts tuh the same thing. I knows yer grateful, but yer compromisin' me jist the same."* Briggs growled, and pushed the quarter back to the clerk.

The clerk shrugged and dropped the quarter into a cigar box.

"No hard feelin's, I hope?" Briggs questioned.

"Nope, yuh done me a favor, an' I 'preciate it." The clerk smiled.

Briggs left the general store, and rolled himself a smoke. The black, and white spotted mutt lay under the boardwalk on the other side of the street, trying to stay in a cooler spot. His tongue was lolling, and he was panting. Briggs figured it would take a lure of major proportions to entice him out from under there.

Under the protection of the hotel porch roof, two old duffers were getting vocal about the rules of the checkers game they were engaged in, and Briggs hoped it wouldn't come to blows. The two old timers looked like a strong wind would blow them both away.

As he strolled down the boardwalk carefully observing his surroundings, he spotted the town marshal coming his way. The man stopped in front of Briggs.

"I unnerstan yer gonna have at it with thet there Carmady feller in the mornin' out by the saloon. Ain't yuh takin' on a bigger load than yuh kin tote?" The marshal chewed on a stub of a cigar, and his brown eyes, shaded by his hatbrim, sparkled with humor.

"Thet's how things are planned. Rough 'n' tumble, no holts barred, an' no weapons. I plan tuh beat 'im tuh death, an' though, tuh yuh, I may seem a bit on the scrawny side, I plan tuh out hustle him, an' use his own strength against him."

"Be thet as it may, mah friend, I don't hold with a lota ruckus in Wolf Point, but long's there's no weapons, Ah'm gonna turn mah head, and wink, as I know fer a fact Carmady runs with a bunch uh cutthroats thet hideout in the hills, an' yuh be keerful, Mister, I am sure Carmady doesn't plan on losin' thet fight. I am gonna tell yuh right now, iffin he comes up with a gun, Ah'll shoot him mah ownself. This here territory would be better off iffin his kind would jist move outa here!" The marshal seemed serious.

Briggs asked, *"Have yuh warned Carmady 'bout it?"*

"Not as yet, but yuh kin put chur cartwheel on the win space, an' bet on uh sure thing, I'm gonna have uh talk with him." The marshals' eyes snapped and he tossed away the soggy cigar stub, turned and walked off down the street.

Briggs stood in the shade with his hat brim pulled low on his forehead, and carefully watched the street, and buildings. With most of the town knowing about the set to coming up the next morning, he didn't think Carmady would shoot him from ambush, but he might join the war of nerves Briggs had begun. One of the geezers in the checker match lost his temper, and flipped the checkerboard upside down, scattering the wooden disks across the veranda of the hotel.

"Har, har, yuh lost again, Abner. Yuh jist don't plan yer moves fur nuff ahead. Gotta be a poor loser, an' tip the board over." The toothless one laughed.

"Yuh sound like uh scrawny rooster crowin'. Yuh know how much yer braggin' gits on mah nerve. Take yer blasted checkerboard an' shove it where the sun don't shine." The other old geezer left in a huff.

Briggs smiled to himself. He could tell they were best of friends, and they'd be back here playing again the next day. The arguing was just part of the game.

The marshal caught up with Carmady in the saloon near noontime.

"Carmady, I don't hold with a big ruckus in mah town, but I'd be run outa the county iffin I asked yuh tuh leave now. As much interest as this here scrap has raised, an' lotsa money has been bet on the outcome, so I'm gonna turn mah head, an' pretend it ain't gonna happen." He stopped to light up a cigar. He had Carmady's attention. *"Thing is I'm gonna insist on one rule, an' thet is no gunplay. I don't want any citizens killed, er wounded by stray bullets. Iffin either one uh yuh pulls iron, I'll shoot him down my ownself. Now we'uns get thet clear?"* The marshal stared into the big man's eyes.

Carmady just nodded, and turned to take a gulp of his whiskey. As the marshal turned to go, Carmady wiped his mouth on the back of his hand, and stewed. What kind of a rough, an' tumble fighter would pull iron on his opponent, anyhow? He remembered the barkeeps' tale of the town bully ready to backshoot the Briggs fella, as he was losing the fight, and he could see where the town marshal was coming from.

"Barkeep, yuh got any lunch here?" He asked.

The bartender reached under the counter, and then placed a pork sandwich, and a boiled potato on a plate in front of Carmady. He wolfed the food, and washed it down with a half glass of whiskey. It would carry him until supper time. He had to admit that tricky Briggs fella had got him somewhat jumpy, what with his sneakin'

round, and pointin' guns in his face, and the man could have probably killed him either time, but he realized the purpose was to put
him on edge, and he tried to ignore the feeling of disaster that stuck
in his craw. Well, he could play tricks, too, and had one in mind, after
he'd seen Briggs sparking that pale eyed waitress in the dining hall.

The dining hall was where Briggs feet took him. It wasn't
crowded, as yet, and he found a place to sit, and wait for Laura to
find him. Find him she did.

"What will it be, Mister Briggs?"

Briggs dearly loved to hear that voice. He gazed into those
pale blue eyes and smiled. *"Beefsteak, taters, beans, an' a wedge of
thet apple pie, with lotsa coffee."* He beamed.

Laura smiled. *"I like a man who knows what he wants, with
no gee, and haw."* She turned, and hurried for the kitchen.

Briggs studied her form, as she was walking away, and knew
in his heart, this was the woman for him. He had never in his life
taken a tumble for a young lady, as he had for this one, and he dearly
hoped she felt the same thing. He'd noticed how her eyes seemed to
soften when she was speaking to him, and maybe, just maybe she did
feel Dan Cupid's arrow. So what, if she did have a twelve year old
daughter? It was a ready made family, and he could learn parenting
with Laura's help.

Briggs gazed about the dining hall, but didn't see any sign
of Carmady. He was slightly startled when someone took the chair
across the table from him. He looked up. It was the town marshal.

*"Carmady has been well warned, about pullin' iron. I toll
him iffin he dragged iron I would shoot him myself, and I'm sure he
understood mah warnin'. Mind iffin I join yuh?"* he asked.

"Be mah guest, marshal." Briggs invited. Laura returned
with Briggs meal and set it on the table.

"Marshal Stalworth, what will you have?" she wondered.
The man stared at what was on the table.

"Whot ever Briggs is havin' looks mighty tasty, why don't

yawl jist bring me the same." Laura returned to the kitchen.

As Briggs began his supper, he asked Marshal Stalworth, *"Do you know Laura well?"*

The man glanced at Briggs. *"Matter uh fact I do, she's mah wife's sister's girl, why duh yuh ask?"*

Briggs shrugged his shoulders, not wanting to admit the real reason. The marshal urged him:

"Yuh must have had a reason tuh ask, now what duh yuh wanta know?"

Briggs squirmed in his chair. *"If yuh must know, marshal, I'm kinda sweet on her.....No, wait, it's more than thet. I've fell fer the lady."* he admitted.

"Yuh know, don't cha, she's got a girl, bout eleven, er twelve years old? Most men wouldn't wanta take on the chore of rasin' uh youngun, an', look it you, who's tuh say yer gonna be alive this time tomorrow." The marshal said.

"All you've said may be true, but yuh know Dan Cupid ain't particular when he shoots them arras uh his, an' I'm feared he done got me, first shot." Briggs admitted.

"Well, she's a growed woman, an iffin yawl kin work somethin' out yuh got mah blessin'" The marshal smiled.

Briggs was somewhat relieved, but hoped the marshal wouldn't just blurt out what he'd said in front of Laura. She appeared and put another meal on the table.

"There you go, Uncle Theodore, enjoy." she smiled at Briggs, as she turned to go back to the kitchen.

"Yup, I kin see you've got it bad, cowboy, yer face lit up like a red lantern." He grinned and dug into his supper.

Briggs leaned back in his chair and sipped on his mug of

coffee. He hadn't thought it had been that obvious and he hadn't felt his face getting hot. Well, maybe, the marshal was just funnin' him. He watched Laura serving other customers, and was struck by the graceful way she moved. He had to admit, to himself, he was falling deeply in love with the lady. He'd only known her a few hours, and was amazed how his emotions were in a turmoil. He'd have to deal with Carmady in the morning, and wondered if he could keep his wits about him, and keep Laura out of his thoughts.

He set his empty mug on the table, and when he looked up, was surprised to see her walking his way, with a smile on her comely face.

"Mr. Briggs," her musical voice delighted him, *"the noon rush is over, and I'm free to go."*

Briggs stood, and left a silver dollar on the table. Briefly he wondered why no man had seized the opportunity to woo this lass, but then there was the little girl. He knew few men would want the responsibility. With her arm through his, he escorted her out the door, and down the street.

"I purely enjoy escortin' yuh home, Laura, and I'm delighted tuh be in yer company. I gotta tell yuh, Ma'am, iffin yuh ain't realized it as yet, I have fell in love with yuh, in jist the few hours I have known yuh." He admitted.

Laura squeezed his arm, and smiled. *"You know I do have a twelve year old daughter, don't you Mr. Briggs?"* She asked seriously.

"I do, and kin see no problem there, Laura. I come from a big family. Six brothers, an' five sisters, so yuh knows I've always been surrounded by a passle uh folks. Mah youngest brother is the reason I gotta kill uh man tomorrow mornin'. It ain't mah nature tuh kill, as a rule, but this viper done kilt Mason. Jist shot 'im down, from ambush without knowin' who he was. He did make uh mistake, an' I know the Good Lord don't hold with killin', but yuh knows blood is thicker un water, an' I am mah brothers keeper." He explained.

"A man must do what he must do, but I sincerely hope you can prevail over this other man, who ever he may be." She answered.

133

They slowly walked to the end of the road, where stood a small three room house. This must be it. *"Thank you, Mr. Briggs, for escorting me to my home, and please don't think me a bold, and brazen hussy, but I would be proud to invite you to join Carrie and myself, for supper here about six of the evening."* She suggested shyly.

Briggs was touched, and felt cheerful, knowing he had found a kindred soul, who was beginning to have feelings for him, in maybe the same way he felt about her.

"I would be proud tuh, Miss Laura. Nothin' would make me happier."

Briggs tipped his hat with a smile, and a warm feeling inside for Laura. She turned, and entered the little house, and Briggs began walking back down the street, not seeing Carmady watching him from behind some brush along the road. 'So, the cowboy was sweet on the little lady.' Carmady laid plans that would definitly give him the edge.

Briggs wished his horse was cured so he wouldn't have to walk everywhere. These boots were not made for walking, and he could feel a sore place on his heel beginning to develop. He made it back to his hotel room without limping like a stove up horse. As he sat on his bed, and pulled off his boots, he discovered the problem. There was a hole worn in his stocking. He knew that darning that spot would make his heel worse, and develop a blister. The best thing he could do now was just keep to his room, and not wear his boots until evening when he was invited to Laura's home for supper. He removed the cartridges from his Colt, took the cylinder out, and inspected the mechanism of the gun to make sure it would perform when needed the most. He'd always taken good care of his gun, and it had never let him down. There were, of course more modern guns to be had, like the .44 Smith & Wesson Russian model, but in his own mind he liked the feel, balance, and reliability of his Walker Colt. It was something he was used to and why change just for the sake of change?

There was a heavy knock on the door. Briggs was in a quandary. His gun lay in pieces on the bed, but then if someone meant him harm they surely wouldn't bother to knock. He got up from the bed, and went to the door. There stood the big woman from room twenty-five. She had a pensive expression on her face.

"Mister, I purely want tuh thank yuh fer not tossin' mah meal ticket outa the winder. Iffin he was tuh git busted up, I don't know what I'd do. I don't hold with the little twerp sneakin' about the hotel of a night, an' prowlin' folk's rooms, but thets the nature of the little varmint. I reckon I cud hogtie him tuh the bedpost, er some such. Anyhow thanks again, an' as I've heard yer gonna go rough 'n tumble with thet Carmady feller, on the morrow, I got a tip fer yuh. Feller thet big, yuh wouldn't think he'd be skeered uh nothin', but thet fool is plumb terrorized by spiders. Kin yuh feature? Makes no never mind, be they itty-bitty, er tarantulas. Jist thought I'd return uh favor." she nodded, and turned to return to her room.

As Briggs closed the door, he wondered how in the world did the woman know about Carmady's fear of spiders? Maybe she'd known him from an earlier time. He sat back down on the bed and cleaned his six-shooter.

Wiping the parts all down with an oily rag, he carefully reassembled, loaded it and placed it back in it's holster. Absently he reached into his shirt pocket, and withdrew the papers and bag of Bull Durham. He rolled himself a cigarette and lit up. He'd been twice in Carmady's face, he knew the man didn't see too well out of his left eye, the man's fear of spiders, and him not knowing Briggs was a lefthander, were all on the plus side.

Carmady outweighed him, was a no holds barred veteran of many fights, probably had a trick or two up his sleeve, and no doubt hit like a mule kick with both fists. He admitted, to himself, he was worried about his chances. Maybe he'd made a basic error in judgement telling Carmady he meant to kill him.

Well, no never mind. What's done, is done. His cigarette burned his finger and he ground it out on the washstand. He palmed his stemwinder, and was astonished to discover the afternoon was gone. It was five-fifteen. Briggs washed up, shaved, put on clean clothes, and combed his hair.

He left his room, and walked down the stairs past the dozing room clerk. The clean socks he'd put on, protected the sore spot on his heel, and made walking a mite easier.

The walk to Laura's house was uneventful, and he hoped she wouldn't mind if he was a few minutes early. He stepped up onto the stoop, and rapped on the door. A thin little girl opened the door, and greeted him with a shy smile.

"You must be Carrie." Briggs smiled in return. *"You show promise of your mother's beauty, young lady."*

The girl curtsied. *"I thank you, Mister Briggs, and welcome to our home."* She stood back to let him enter.

The child had been raised to be polite, and he noticed she had the same pale blue eyes, but her hair was a shade darker than her mother's. He removed his Stetson, and Carrie reached for it. She hung it on a shaker peg she had to stand on tip toe to reach.

"Please sit down Mister Briggs, what would you like to hear?" She asked.

He found a chair, but had no idea what the girl meant, until she seated herself at the upright piano.

"Whatever pleases you, Carrie." He replied.

She turned to the keyboard, and began a lively tune he recognized as "Buffalo Gal" followed by "The Rose of Alabama". When he looked toward the kitchen door, Laura was standing there watching her daughter proudly.

"Supper's on the table." She announced.

Carrie stood, and walked toward the kitchen. Briggs stood, and followed. He waited until the mother and daughter were seated, and sat on the remaining chair. Laura passed the filled bowls of food-boiled potatoes, vegatable soup, pork, and sour kraut, fried chicken and fresh sliced peaches. The coffee was strong and black.

"I must compliment yuh on the fine meal, Miss Laura"

Briggs pushed back away from the table and rolled a cigarette. This was the life, sitting at the supper table, enjoying an after supper cigarette and the admiring glances of Laura, and her daughter.

After the dishes were cleared, they sat and talked about everything that came to mind. Three hours passed, but they didn't notice. Finally Briggs said his goodbyes, stepped out onto the stoop and let his eyes adjust to the dark.

He listened to the night sounds and didn't hear anything that would disturb the evening tranquility. He stepped off the porch and began his trip back to his hotel.

Nearly three hundred yards from Laura's house his eyes caught a furtive movement he couldn't identify. It seemed to him to be a solid manshape. He didn't break step or indicate he'd seen anything, but kept on walking toward downtown. He found a spot where the brush was heavy and slipped into it.

Briggs turned to watch the house and was rewarded when the shape revealed itself against the white clapboard. He quietly retraced his steps.

Could it be the woman's husband returning from the Yukon? He didn't think so. The more he thought about it the more he believed it was Carmady. The man had seen him talking to Laura in the dining hall. More than likely he had planned something evil. Well, Briggs could make evil plans too. He stepped closer to the house. He was careful, putting himself in line with brush, and trees so as not reveal himself. He heard the hinge creak of the back door opening, and shortly thereafter a muffled gasp, cut short.

Briggs stepped carefully to the back door, which was standing ajar, and into the house. The sounds of a quiet struggle, and the rush of air through a nose, like a mouth was covered, and someone could not draw in enough air.

Briggs quietly drew his Colt from its' holster, and feeling carefully with his toes, stepped closer to where the sounds were coming from. A muffled whimper, and a sharp, harsh whispered warning,

"Shut up!" It had sounded like Carmady's voice, but he couldn't be sure.

"Mother?" The girl's voice startled Briggs, and he was sure it had the same effect on the struggling Carmady.

"Mother, what's happening? why don't you answer me?"

Briggs was sure the girl suspected something was wrong. The girl lit a lamp, and began walking slowly toward the dining room where Briggs could finally see what was occuring. It was Carmady and he held the struggling Laura against the wall. Usually Briggs was able to keep cool under stressful circumstances, but observing

Laura being mauled in her own home, was more than his temper would stand for.

He stepped up, and smashed the bigger man behind the ear with his Colt putting all his strength into the blow. Not caring if he killed him. Carmady dropped like a sack of wheat, without a sound, pulling Laura with him.

Carrie entered the room fully, bathing the scene in the pale lampglow. Briggs helped Laura to her feet. She put her arms about his neck, and clung to him, shaking like a wind blown wheatstalk. He holstered his gun, and held Laura.

"Who is that man, Mister Briggs, and why was he rough-housing my mother?" Carrie wanted some answers.

"Carrie, I feel uts' mah fault puttin' you, an' yer mom in danger. This man, and I have a difference tuh settle, an' this was something he felt he had to do to get an edge on me. Uts' a cowards' way of gettin' at me. I hope I kilt him!" Briggs answered.

Carmady hadn't moved since he'd fallen. Carrie set the lamp on the table, and came over to join Briggs, and Laura.

"Mother, are you alright?" she asked.

Laura reached for her, and hugged her with one arm. *"Mister Briggs I hate to think what would have happened if you hadn't come back."* She was still trembling.

"Don't think about it, Laura, its' all over now, an' yer safe." He tried to calm her.

A low moan escaped from the fallen Carmady. He was finally coming around. Carmady sat up holding his head.

"Yuh got whot yuh deserved, Carmady, consider yerself lucky yuh got a thick skull. This business was betwix you, an' me, an' yuh had no cause tuh hassle innocent people. Thet's yer main downfall, yuh don't gather all the facts afore yuh go off half cocked, an' git some people what had nothin' tuh do with our fight involved. Now yuh drag yer carcuss on outa here afore I lose mah temper, an' shoot

yuh down like the mad dog thet yuh are!" Briggs told him.

Carmady looked back at him with pure hate glittering in his pain dulled eyes. Without a word the big man staggered erect and left through the back door.

"The man is a backshootin', bounty huntin' coward thet always gotta have a edge over whoever he's up against. He kilt mah brother, Mason, from ambush thinkin' it was somebody else, but I ain't cuttin' him no slack, an' mean to do him in tommarraw." Briggs explained.

"A man must do what he must do, Mister Briggs, but I wouldn't want you to get slain yourself." Laura looked concerned. He noticed Carrie was showing concern too.

"Ah've got a lot tuh live fer now. Meanin' yuh, an' Carrie, an' takin' care uh yuh both. I would be proud tuh marry yuh, Miss Laura, iffin yu'd have me." Briggs blurted out. Laura looked curiously at him.

"I didn't know you felt that way about us, Mr. Briggs. You've only known us a few hours. Do you know how hard it is to raise a youngster? Do you know what a temper I have when I get mad? How can you support a family? I'd be delighted to be your wife, and although I can't speak for Carrie, I know she needs a father too. Yes, oh yes, I'll marry you Mr. Briggs!" she exclaimed.

"Me too, I want you to be my father, Mr. Briggs, I'll honor, and respect you until the day I die. I like you a lot." The girl gushed.

Briggs pulled Laura to him, and with arms about her waist, he kissed her firmly on the lips. Yes, Briggs was totally in love with her. He broke the kiss and gazed into her pale blue eyes.

"I'd best be uh hoofin' it back to mah hotel room, an' git some sleep fer tuh be rested up fer what I gotta do in the mornin'" He admitted.

"You're welcome to spend the night here." Laura said.

"As temptin' as thet offer is, I know in mah heart it would be best fer all concerned fer me tuh leave." Briggs kissed Laura again, and left by the front door.

The walk back to his hotel was uneventful. Briggs was wary, and watched every shadow that might have concealed Carmady. He grinned, hoping Carmadys' headache was so overpowering, he wouldn't get any sleep. He suspected he'd finally cut the bigger man down to size, being in his face twice today, and showing up back at Lauras' house when he was least expected. He wondered what Carmady had in mind mauling Laura like he did. Sure, it was to get to him, but how? kidnapping her? beating, and punching her into unconsciousness? He would probably never know. He entered the hotel, and climbed the stairs. His room door stood partly open. Briggs pulled his Colt from his holster, and eased into his lamplit room. It was the town marshal sitting on his bed.

"Marshal?" Briggs holstered his gun.

"Uh careful man yuh are, Briggs, an' that's good. I've been waitin' tuh give yuh some news since yuh are becomming a close friend of mah niece. I've received some news of the death of Laura's husband. He was kilt, as I had suspected, fer the claim he'd found some color in, an' fer the gold he'd collected from it. I will be the one tuh break the news tuh her, but I wanted yuh tuh know firsthand, yer chances er somewhat better as of now." The marshal explained.

Briggs took off his gunbelt, and hung it on the bedstead. *"Marshal I done asked Miss Laura tuh marry up with me, an' she done said 'yes'. I hope yer news don't crimp up our plans."* he admitted.

The older man stood, and offered his hand to Briggs. *"Congratulations, son, yuh couldn't have made a better choice,"* he shook Briggs hand, *"she don't have no living father, an' I would be proud tuh give her away at yer hitchin', thet is iffin yawl will have me."* He grinned and stood to leave. As he walked out the door he turned and winked at Briggs.

BAD NEWS
Chapter 6

Briggs bade the man a good night and closed the door behind him. He didn't know how Laura was going to take the news of the death of her husband. He knew she suspected he had met his demise. The actual fact though, was a different story all together, and might change her thinking. He blew out the lamp and undressed slowly. Slipping his Colt under the pillow, he relaxed with his hands locked behind his head and thought the day to come.

During the night, as Briggs slept fitfully, an event took place that was to change the lives of many people in Wolf Point. On his last round of the town, marshal Stalworth discovered Carmady drunk and asleep against the front of the Longbranch saloon. As he leaned over to help the man to his feet, Carmady, with an oath, pulled his six-gun, and shot the marshal dead.

Carmady, in his miserable state, didn't realize the gravity of his rash act. A small crowd quickly gathered, and there was talk of a lynching. Marshal Stalworth had been a strict, but fair lawman. He had the respect of most of the townsmen. Carmady was roped up and dragged to the small jail. Carmady in his drunken stupor, stared angrily at them as the cell door slammed, and was locked. The decision on what was to be done with the murderous outlaw was left until morning.

As the sun rose, and the word spread, a swell of anger overcame the entire town, and an angry lynch mob did indeed form, heading en masse toward the jail. The mutter of the angry crowd awoke Briggs. He stepped to the window, and watched. He recognized the intentions of the rowdy crowd and quickly dressed. He hurried down the stairs, and out into the street. He was more or less a stranger in the town and knew he could have little influence, but he had to try. He hurried ahead of the main part of them and reached the jail first. He turned to face them, and raised his hands:

"Folks, think a what yer about tuh do and search yer souls. Duh yuh want tuh have this man's life on yer conscience? I'm a stranger here, but I kin tell yer mostly good folks jist caught up in a fit uh anger, an' will regret whot yer 'bout tuh do, in the future. Nows' the time tuh think, an' decide." Briggs lowered his arms and gazed at the angry crowd.

Some of them shuffled their feet with indecision, but the larger portion of the group still pressed forward, and elbowed Briggs out of their way at the doorway. As they entered the jail house, they were greeted by the pathetic sight of Carmady sleeping it off in the cell. He had vomited all over himself and wet his pants. A roach crawled across his face and settled on his lower lip. Carmady slept on.

Eventually, someone yelled, *"Let the law take care of it!"* And with that, the crowd's anger relented.

The only trouble now was that there wasn't any law in Wolf Point. This was taken care of in a hurried meeting with the mayor and some of the leading business men. They met in the mayor's home and decided to appoint a new town marshal at once.

Briggs was eating his breakfast in the dining hall, and thinking about the events that had transpired in the last few hours. His battle with Carmady was now out of the question for the present. With the brute secure in the jail cell his revenge would have to be put on hold. He looked up to see six men heading for his table. It made his pulse quicken. What did they have in mind? The old duffer with the white goat whiskers seemed to be in charge.

"Mister Briggs?" the man began.

Briggs swallowed the fried taters he'd been chewing. *"I'm Briggs Clayborn,"* he answered, wiping his mouth on a napkin.

"Sorry to disturb yore morning meal, but I'm Mayor Childress, this is Henry Bishop, Thomas Post, Warner Robbins, Alvin Dusek, and this is Whitney Chance. These gentlemen are some of the leading merchants, and we've come to ask if you would consider the job of town marshal."

This offer came as a surprise to Briggs. It was about the last thing on his mind, but when he considered it the thought came to him. If he planned to wed, a means of supporting his family was in all probability a first on his list. He decided to accept their proposal.

"Gentlemen, I will accept yer offer with one condition, an' thet is yawl attend the forthcomin' weddin' of one of yer most hand-

some women, and mahself at a date tuh be named in the near future. I have fell in love, an' have ask Miss Laura Stevens tuh be mah wife." Briggs announced.

"Congratulations, Mr. Clayborn." The mayor said and all the men present shook his hand.

The mayor handed Briggs the silver marshal's badge and watched as he pinned it on his shirt front. Briggs left a dollar on the table, and walked to the marshal's office at the jail. He stepped back to the cells and stared at Carmady.

"Well, bounty hunter, yuh done got yerself in a world uh trouble. I bin appointed town marshal, Carmady, an' since our differences can't be settled as planned, Ah'll haft tuh be satisfied tuh see yuh hang. Ut's too bad we'uns will never know jist who the better man is."

"Jist take off thet badge, an' open the cell door, an' we'll see!" Carmady muttered belligerently.

"Hush up Carmady, yuh know I can't. Yer breakfast wull be comin' purty soon, but iffin yuh want a chance tuh wash up, I'll push a wash basin, some soap, an' a towel under the door. Ah'll git yuh a clean shirt too. Where's yer horse?" Briggs asked.

Carmady just stared at him for a spell, and then spoke. *"Yer a decent man, Clayborn, an' I know I done wrong lettin' whiskey git the upper hand. Mah horse is at the livery, an' the soap, an' water is 'preciated."*

Briggs turned, and left the jail. He walked over to the general store, and picked out a flannel shirt big enough to fit Carmady. He paid for it out of his pocket, and returned to the jail. He pumped some water into the wash basin, got the soap, and a towel. He pushed the basin, and soap under the cell door, hung the towel, and new shirt through the bars. He went back, sat at the desk, and opened the drawer. Carmady's skinning knife, gunbelt, and six shooter lay there. The gun was a Remington, worn, but well taken care of. He pushed out the rod, and removed the cylinder.

Of the five rounds, one had been fired. The one that had

killed Marshal Stalworth. He replaced the cylinder and rod, then dropped the gun back in the drawer.

"Marshal?"

A young lad called from the doorway. He was carrying a napkin covered tray. Briggs stood, and examined the food, and then took it from the boy, and walked back to the cell. Carmady was just drying off. He hung the towel through the bars, and reached for the new shirt. He donned it and buttoned up, pushing the wash basin under the cell door with his foot.

"Got yer breakfast here, Carmady, jist step back, an' I'll slide it under the door."

The man stepped back to the rear of the small cell and Briggs pulled the wash basin out of the way, all the time watching Carmady carefully. He pushed the food under the cell door, and took the wash basin, and soap out the back door, flinging the dirty water in the weeds. He returned to the cell.

"Carmady, I wanted tuh kill yuh, fer bushwhackin' mah brother, but the circuit judge wull be ridin' in here Monday, an' yuh'll git a fair trial, which is more than mah brother got. Iffin I sound bitter, ut's because I am. I feel cheated. Cheated cause I didn't git tuh use the spider bit on yuh." He was surprised at the sudden look of terror that was reflected in Carmady's eyes.

"Whot cha know 'bout spiders?" Carmady asked nervously.

"I know yer mortally terrified of em." Briggs answered. Carmady stared at him.

"There's only one way yuh coulda discovered thet, and I din't know thet hefty shrew was in this territory."

"Yup, an' she's got herself a skinny pup of uh man unner her thumb. She put me wise 'cause I din't maim 'im whin I had the right tuh. She was grateful I din't toss 'im outa the winder, and bust 'im up." Briggs grinned.

"I swear, Clayborn, yuh done won the war uh nerves, an'
I'm not so sure I could uh whupped yuh. I gotta say again I'm plumb
sorry I done kilt yer brother by mistake, an' maybe seein' me hang
will atone fer it. I would like tuh clear muh slate afore I meets mah
Maker, an' request the services of uh preacher man on the day yuh
plans tuh hang me." Carmady spoke sincerely.

"It'll be arranged." Briggs answered, leaving the cell area.
He sat back down at the desk again for a short while, and then got up
to walk to Lauras' home, and relate to her the news that Marshal
Stalworth had for her.

Bad News Travels Fast
Chapter 7

As Carrie answered his knock. She smiled. *"Hi, Mr. Briggs, my moms' at work if you wanted to see her."*

"Yore right, I plumb fergot she'd be workin', but ut's nice tuh see yuh, Carrie, an' good mornin' to yuh." He tipped his hat, and turned to leave.

"Uncle Theodore got killed last night, did you know about it, Mr. Briggs?" Carrie asked.

He turned back to face the young girl. *"Yes, I did, Carrie, an' they done 'ppointed me the town marshal in 'is place. I also should tell yuh yore uncle Ted tole me las night thet I have gotta break the news tuh yer mom thet yore paw has been kilt for shore up there in the Yukon Territory. I know you an' yer mom had suspected thet was the case, but I know it hurts tuh hear the fact. Was yuh close tuh yer uncle, Carrie?"* Briggs asked the girl.

"I liked him. He'd always bring me candy, and such when he came to visit, but we really never saw very much of him." she answered.

Carrie didn't seem to be really broken up about the man's death, or maybe she was too young to understand the fact of it.

Briggs left the small house, and walked back to the main street. His heel was getting sore again with all this walking. An idea hit him at that time. Why not use Carmady's horse? The man in jail sure didn't need it and wasn't going to use it. He cut across between the feed store, and the gunsmiths' building taking a short cut to the livery barn.

The hostler was pitching hay down from the mow, and didn't hear Briggs' first greeting.

"Hello, up there!" he shouted louder.

The hostler peered over the edge of the opening and leaned on his hay fork.

"Good day tuh yuh," the man replied, still staring down, *"whot kin I do fer yuh?"*

"I bin 'ppointed town marshal, an' needs a horse, an' since I got Carmady locked up in jail, I'm gonna use his'n until mah own horse is done healed up."

"Makes no never mind tuh me jist so's somebody pays fer his keep." The hostler replied. *"It's the chestnut with the blaze on 'is forehead. Purty horse, but with thet Oklahoma circle K brand on 'im I suspect he's stolen. Saddles' there on the bench, 'long with the blanket."*

Briggs stopped to pet the horse on the neck, before he led him out of the stall. It was a clean cut sturdy looking horse he guessed to be about seven or eight years old. He threw the blanket over the broad back, and then heaved the saddle on. He cinched it up tight, and mounted. Briggs rode the horse out of the livery barn, and down the street to the dining hall. After dismounting, he tied the reins to the hitchrack, and entered the hall. Briggs removed his Stetson, and gazed about, trying to see Laura. It was nearing noon, and the kitchen was abustle with activity.

Laura spotted him first, and came out of the kitchen.

"Mr. Briggs, you're too early for dinner, but I'm glad to see you." She lit up the dining hall with her smile.

Briggs heart did a flip-flop when he heard her voice, and he developed an ache in his chest. Seen through his eyes, she was so beautiful.

"Laura I got some bad news fer yuh. I don't really wanta be the one tuh break it to yuh, but I ain't got uh choice."

"I know, uncle Ted got killed last night." She replied.

"Last night yer uncle Ted stopped by mah room, an' tole me he'd got proof yer husbans' body done been found in the Yukon Territory an' he was gonna tell yuh this mornin', but yuh know whot happened las' night. The mayor done 'ppointed me tuh be the town marshal, and it was up tuh me tuh tell yuh."

Briggs looked into Laura's pale blue eyes, and watched a tear trickle down her cheek. Laura grabbed onto Briggs and held him tight.

"I loved that man, and he's the father to my daughter. I had hopes he'd come back, rich or not. I wanted him to come home, but when I didn't hear from him for more than a year, I suspected he'd met with his Maker. The actual fact, though, dashes all hope, you know?, and Carrie, an, me will grieve for him." she looked up into Briggs face.

"This doesn't change anything between us, Briggs, I'm in love with you, and still want to be your wife. Just give me a short while to adjust to the fact of my widowhood." She explained.

Briggs held her until she turned to go back to her duties in the kitchen.

As Briggs turned to leave, a commotion developed outside the hall, and three shots were fired. He hurried outside in time to see the horse he'd been riding, and three others gallop out of town. Carmady had been busted out of jail by three of his cronies. He wanted to follow, but with no horse, and the responsibility of the town of Wolf Point and commitment to Laura, it wasn't possible. He hoped their paths would cross again before the outlaw got caught, and hanged.

OUTLAW'S FLIGHT
Chapter 8

Carmady was both surprised, and elated when old Bascome had appeared at his cell window.

"Whin yuh didn't come back with mah whiskey, I tole the boys yuh was probly settin' in jail. I convinced em tuh come 'long an' bust yuh out." The old geezer grinned.

They tied two horses to the rear window bars, and pulled them out of their settings. Carmady was out and running before the dust cleared. He spotted his horse tied in front of the dining hall and made a beeline for him. His companions fired a few shots to keep the townspeople at bay, and the four of them rode out of Wolf Point like the mill tails of hell. After a mile at a full gallop, confident that they weren't being followed, they slowed down to a lope. Carmady ask for paper and Bull Durham from one of his companions. As he rolled his smoke, he warned,.

"Well, gents, I now got a price on mah head. I done shot, an' kilt the town marshal. So theys gonna be hot on mah trail right soon now. Iffin yuh wanna split up an' go separate ways, I'll unnerstan."

"Don't sweat it, Carmady, we uns' all got a price on us. I guess we'd be best movin' tuh a cooler climate, where things ain't so hot fer us." Charlie Goodyear grinned. *"I allus wanted tuh see whot Canada looked like, how 'bout it fellers?"*

They all nodded in agreement, and turned their horses North. Carmady knew he'd have to find a gun, gunbelt, rifle, ammo, and a good skinning knife somewhere along the trail. Killing was easy, and a lone pilgrim with the right equipment wouldn't be hard to find. They rode North the rest of the day, and near dark found a well used cave in the side of a rolling hill that would serve for an overnight shelter.

Bascome scouted about for some firewood, as the other outlaws dug into their saddlebags for coffee, sidemeat, jerky, and beans. Later they sat about the dying fire, and jawed about the trip they were undertaking, the food they would need, and the best way to find a place to hole up in during the daytime. It was a moonless night, and after the fire died, they rolled themselves in their blankets.

As they slept, and their hobbled horses grazed nearby, a mountain lion watched the steeds chomping at the grass. With her tail a twitch and a growl deep in her throat, she crept closer. One of the horses was separated from the other three, by nearly a hundred yards. This was the meal the mountain lion had been stalking from down wind. She crept closer, and then tensed, as the horse raised his head. His ears erect, and nostrils flared trying to catch scent, or sound of a danger he suspected was near. He didn't detect his peril until the big cat sprung at him. In his panic he tried to gallop, but his hobble pitched him to the ground.

The horse whinnied in panic as the lion landed on him, but the sound was cut short when the cat held and slashed him. The other horses moved as quickly as their hobbles would permit. They would put as much distance as possible between themselves, and their luckless companion. One of the outlaws had muttered and turned over at the sound of the horses death cry, but didn't wake up.

When the rising sun touched the hilltops, Carmady was first up. He shook out his boots, pulled his britches on, buttoned his shirt, and donned his Stetson. He stepped to the cave entrance, and stretched.

"Hey! our horses er gone!" His yell brought the other men to their feet.

"Whatcha mean, gone?" Charlie Goodyear asked.

"Look fer yerself, Charlie, they ain't in sight nowhere. It 'ppears somthin' is layin' there by the underbrush, an' I suspect ut's one uh them!" Carmady pointed. *"Mountain lion, I recon, got one of em, an' the others hobbled off, it's gonna be a long walk, an' I guess I might as well git started."*

"Here," Charlie offered his six-shooter, *"yuh might need is."*

Carmady nodded, and tucked the gun through his belt. He walked toward the dead horse and discovered it was Chet Mowery's horse. He noted the unmistakable tracks of a mountain lion. He circled until he found the hobbled horses tracks, and followed.

He walked for over an hour, but was brought up short by the smell of woodsmoke. He discovered a campfire with a battered coffee pot sitting on a rock at the edge of the blaze. A ground hitched horse munched at the short grass nearby. There was an empty bedroll near the fire, but he could see no sign of the horses' owner. Carmady shouted. *"Hello, the campfire."* He was startled when a voice spoke to him from somewhere behind him.

"I got a rifle pointin' right at yuh, Mister, whot yuh want?" It was a female voice trying to speak in a low alto tone. Carmady started to turn.

"Stop turnin', an' answer mah question." The voice ordered. Carmady shifted his weight to the other foot.

"Ah'm huntin' three hobbled horses whot wandered away las' night whin they was spooked by a mountain lion, an' I smelled yer campfire. I was hopin' yud have a cup uh coffee leftover, as I bin walkin' 'bout a hour."

"I saw them horses, an' yer 'bout fifteen minutes behind em. Gimmie 'bout tin more minutes, an' I'll round up em fer yuh. Ya'll go set by the fire, an' pour yerself some coffee."

Carmady gratefully walked to the campfire, and sat on a log. He reached for the coffee pot, and then poured some coffee into the tin cup that was sitting on a flat rock. He looked up to see an older woman strolling toward the fire. She did indeed carry a Winchester repeater under her arm. Carmady blew on the hot coffee, and took a small sip.

"I surmise you an' a couple uh other cowboys will be afoot les yuh kin ketch them horses." She supposed.

Carmady didn't see any reason to tell her there were four of them. *"Thet's 'bout the way it stacks up, ma'am, an' I do 'ppreciate yuh ridin' off after em thet way."*

"Hmmmph, I know how a body is helpless in this country without a horse. I bin there a time er two mah ownself."

She sat across the fire from him, and poured herself some of the coffee. He let her finish her coffee and then drew his borrowed six-shooter. The woman was shot right between the eyes.

"Shouldn't trust nobody, woman, a soul lives longer jist puttin' trust in his own abilities." He explained to the dead woman. He was already wanted for murder, and another wasn't going to make him any guiltier. Besides he needed her horse, and rifle.

He bent over, and searched her body. He found a gun, gunbelt, and ammo for the rifle. Too bad she didn't carry a skinning knife too. This camp was in a grove of trees, and the body probably wouldn't be found for a spell. Carmady took the reins of the horse, and heaved himself into the saddle. He put the Winchester into the boot and rode after the hobbled horses. He collected them in just a few minutes, took their hobbles off and led them back the way he had come.

"Gotcher self a horse, an' outfit. We heard the shot, an' figgered yud found some ranny by his self." Charlie Goodyear grinned.

Carmady dismounted from the horse and returned the six-shooter to Charlie. *"Thanks fer the loan of yer gun, Charlie."*

He wasn't about to tell them it was a woman he'd killed. While he'd been gone the other men had rolled up their blankets and tied up their bedrolls. Bascome tossed Carmady's to him and they all mounted. They stuck to the trees and brush as they traveled. The going was tougher but there was less chance of meeting anyone.

The game trails were a big help to keep the horses from tiring. Then, late in the afternoon, they came upon a small town with a trading post at the edge. Carmady went alone to the trading post, as the other outlaws hung back in the woods and smoked.

Carmady wandered about the store looking at blankets, bolts of cloth, farm implements, tools, guns, and ammunition.

"Kin I help, yuh?" The old codger behind the counter asked.

"I need a skinnin' knife, and some .44 Colt ammunition, couple uh boxes." He replied.

The proprietor placed three different knives on the counter, along with two boxes of .44 ammunition. One of the knives Carmady didn't even consider. It was cheaply made. He picked up the drop point Green River knife, and examined it closely. It was similar to the one the town marshal had taken from him. The other knife was a Case, and was formed more along the lines of a fillet knife, and too thin for his liking.

"Got a sheath fer this here Green River knife?"

The man reached back on a shelf and then laid a leather sheath on the counter.

"How much fer the knife, sheath, and bullets, and oh yeah, I need couple sacks uh Bull Durham, an' some papers, an' a sack uh coffee." He added.

The man put the papers, tobacco, and coffee on the counter. He then added up the total on the back of a paper sack.

"Four dollars, and a dime will do it."

Carmady dug into his pocket, and laid a five dollar gold piece on the counter. That just about did it for his ready cash. The woman he'd killed hadn't been carrying any. He'd have to find a new supply before long. He got ninety cents in change and turned to leave the store.

"Mister?"

Carmady froze, his heart hammering in his chest.

"Mister, yuh fergot yer sheath fer yore knife."

Carmady turned and accepted the sheath the man held out to him. *"Thanks."* He muttered and left the trading post.

He mounted his horse and headed into the woods where his companions waited. He pushed the knife into its' sheath, and threaded it onto his belt. Putting the two boxes of ammo into the saddlebags, he joined his companions.

"Yuh fellers wanta brew up some coffee, I jist got a sack."

"Sounds good, Carmady, it's near time tuh hunt up a overnight spot anyhow." Bascome advised, and they loped north again.

They found a cleared spot amid the fir trees near a stream. There were old campfire ashes and some empty tin cans scattered about. It was getting dark as they lit a fire and prepared for a meal. They sat around the fire waiting for the water to boil and the side meat to fry. Charlie Goodyear had opened a can of beans with his knife and dished them up in a tin plate which he placed at the edge of the fire to warm.

"Hello, the camp fire."

They were startled by the nearby voice, and in unison reached for their guns.

"I done smelled yer side meat fryin', and it made mah mouth water. Duh yuh mind iffin I join yuh? I done brought some fresh deer meat along yuh kin roast." The voice sounded hopeful.

"Come on up tuh the fire with nothin' in yer hands, but the deer meat then." Mowrey warned, holstering his six-shooter.

A buckskin clad, middle-aged man appeared in the circle of firelight. He appeared to be a trapper, or buffalo hunter. He laid the deer meat on a flat rock, and joined them holding his empty hands out to the fire. Not that it was cold, but he wanted to show them he was indeed unarmed. Bascome skewered the deer meat on some green sticks and poked the ends of the sticks into the ground around the flames.

"Names' Wolters, iffin it makes any difference, an' I'm on mah way tuh Canada. You gents comin' er goin'?" he inquired. Charlie Goodyear looked the man over carefully.

"We're goin', an iffin yuh got a horse, an' these other gents don't have no objection, yer welcome tuh ride along."

The other men nodded in agreement. Wolters pulled a pipe

out of his pocket, and loaded it with tobacco. After he'd tamped it tight with his thumb, he stuck a twig into the flames, and lit up.

"Found a dead woman by a campfire a few miles back thet way," he jerked his head in the direction they had come, *"seems she was a Cattlemen's Association agent 'ccording tuh her wallet. Musta poked her nose in somewhere thet rubbed some rustlers the wrong way, er whatever. I mahself don't hold with killin' nobody, specially a woman, but some rannys ain't so choosey. Don't make no nevermind. I was jist makin' conversation, anyhoo."* He puffed on his pipe.

Carmady was uncomfortable with this disclosure. He hadn't thought the body would have been found so soon. Charlie Goodyear was staring at him strangely. He shifted around and looked Charlie in the eye.

"I know whot yer thinkin' Charlie, but yer dead wrong, I wouldn't shoot no woman." He lied with a straight face. Knowing how touchy most western men were about any woman being harmed in any way. He didn't want to be placed in that category, even though it was true.

Goodyear relaxed somewhat, but still carried a suspicious look on his face. The side meat, and beans were done, and the coffee water was boiling. Bascome dropped a handful of ground coffee beans in the pot, and poured a cup of cold water in to settle the grounds. They all got their tin plates, and cups, and gathered round the fire. Bascome dished up the side meat and beans, and poured the coffee.

The men ate without conversation. Each with his own thoughts, about the dead woman back along the trail. Goodyear figured Carmady was capable of the deed, but was willing to give him the benefit of doubt. Bascome thought Carmady had more sense than to shoot a woman, and he believed him. Chet Mowery was a suspicious man by nature, and he thought the man was guilty. Wolters had no doubt. He had been close when he heard the shot, and left his horse hidden while he crept up on foot.

He'd seen Carmady leaning over the woman, going through her clothes. Knowing there was nothing he could do, and also knowing there were three other men, he waited until Carmady had mounted, and ridden after the horses. Later he'd found the wallet with the Cattlemen's Association card in it. He'd waited around, and had given the woman a decent burial. Letting the foursome get a big lead, he began to follow. He too had stopped at the trading post and bought the deer haunch he'd given to them.

The deer meat was done and Carmady cut slices off the haunch and passed them around the circle. He also had his suspicions. Who was Wolters? Had he been following them, or was it just a chance meeting? He looked the part, but was he really a trapper on his way to Canada?

After supper, and with bellies full, they sat about the fire, and passed the bottle. Unknown to the others Wolters, didn't have any of the whiskey. He faked it, and then passed the bottle along. He didn't trust any of these men... especially Carmady. It had been a full bottle and the four men were mellow after the bottle was empty. They unrolled their bedrolls, and placed them around the fire. Wolters did the same, making sure he was next to Carmady.

After a while there were snores coming from the four whiskey imbibers, and Wolters believed they were in their deepest sleep. He carefully arose, and bent over Carmady. He thumped him solidly over the head with a small log, and then dragged man, and bedroll together far from the fire. There he bound, and gagged the man and saddled his and Carmadys' horse. The real chore was wrestling the big man over his horse, and tying his hands, and feet underneith. He was sweating profusly when the job was done. Leading Carmadys' horse with the owner draped over the saddle, he turned south. Back in the direction he'd come earlier in the day. The easy part had been accomplished, and now the hard part was beginning.

Getting Carmady back to Wolf Point to face trial. Would the other three outlaws follow, and try to take Carmady back, or would they indeed hightail it for Canada? He believed the stigma of associating with a woman killer would speed their way north. At least two of them were skeptical about the man's innocence. He'd read it in their eyes around the campfire.

Wolters was a deputy sheriff who had been sent to bring Carmady back for the killing of the town marshal. Dead, or alive if he could, and he'd vowed to do his best. Carmady groaned, and stirred. When he tried to move, he discovered he was bound, and gagged. He knew then why he had been suspicious of that Wolters fellow. He had no doubt where he was headed.

A BAD PENNY TURNS UP

Chapter 9

Briggs wasted no time in notifing the sheriff about Carmadys' escape, and a deputy had quickly gone after the outlaws. To him the other three didn't matter. He would see the murderer hang even if he had to quit his marshals' job and track the man down himself.

The sheriff had assured him the deputy he sent after them would, without a doubt, return with the man he'd been sent after. He spent half a day repairing the broken bars of the jail. The services of the blacksmith were required to get the bars heated, and hammered back straight again. A mason was hunted up to re-mortar the opening and reset the bars solidly.

Briggs had no idea when the deputy would return with his prisoner, but wanted the jail to be ready to hold him. He watched as the mason troweled morter around the bars. It would, in all likelyhood, take a full twenty-four hours to harden, and longer to set solid.

Briggs walked over to the Longbranch saloon, and ordered a whiskey. The bartender set the half full glass in front of him on the polished bar.

"Hear any news about Carmady, er the other outlaws what busted 'im outa jail? You mighta best let em lynch 'im, an' then there wouldn't be no problem."

Briggs swollowed some of his whiskey, and set the glass back down. *"Maybe so, but I don't hold with killin' a man by stretchin' his neck with a rope 'for he gits a trial. Lemme ask yuh, yuh ever seen a man hang by lynchin? It ain't a purty sight. A proper hangin' breaks a fellers neck, and ut's over quick, but when he gits lynched he strangles, and kicks, an' his face turns purple, an his eyes bug out. Nope, ain't a sight yuh wanta see."* Briggs explained.

"He deserves tuh die slow. Din't he shoot yer brother, an' kill the town marshal? He din't give them a fair chance, why shouldn't he die chokin' an' kickin'?" The bartender growled. He had been wiping the same spot on the bar for five minutes as they talked about it.

"I know, 'A eye fer an eye, an' a tooth fer a tooth' sez so in the Bible, but he's gonna hang proper. The sheriff done sent his best mantracker after him. I suspect we uns be seein' em for long." Briggs told the man. He dropped a quarter on the bar, and walked back out into the late afternoon sun-drenched street. The shadows were long, and pointing east. Briggs pulled the brim of his Stetson low on his forehead, and looked west up the street. A lone rider loped down the far side of the road raising little swirls of dust. He rode an all black horse with the ease of an experienced horseman who spent many hours in the saddle. Although the horse showed the weariness of a long ride, he still stepped with a lively gait.

"Well, I never 'spected tuh see yuh with a badge, young feller." The voice was familiar, but Briggs couldn't see the man's face with the sun in his eyes.

"Yer careless, boy, I coulda pulled iron, an' kilt yuh. Iffin yer gonna be a law dog, yuh gotta be more careful."

Briggs shaded his eyes with his hand, and laughed. It was Bishop. His oldest brother.

"Did yuh find the man who kilt Mason? An' did yuh make it even?" Bishop asked.

"Git offa yer horse, Bish, an' les have a drink, an' I'll tell yuh all 'bout it." Briggs offered.

"Best invite I've had all week, Briggs." He laughed, and dismounted. He tied the reins to the hitchrack, and accompanied his brother into the Longbranch.

The bartender looked up in surprise to see Briggs return so soon.

"Set em up, barkeep, this heres' mah brother Bishop." He stated.

The bartender nodded and set a half full-bottle on the bar along with two clean glasses. Briggs poured both glasses half full,

■158

and went on to explain, *"I done tracked thet Carmady feller tuh here in Wolf Point, but he'd bin hidin' out in the hills until Thursday night, an' I braced 'im in the dinin' hall, an' tole 'im I was gonna beat 'im tuh death. He got drunk las night an' kilt the town marshal. The townspeople put him in the jail, an' 'ppointed me marshal. His amigos done busted 'im outa his cell, and tooken off north. The sheriff sent his mantracker after 'im, an' we uns are waitin' fer 'im tuh come back inta town."*

"Then whot?" Bishop wanted to know.

"The circuit judge will be here Monday, an' find him guilty, an' he'll hang. One thing I'm sorry fer, I'll never git the pleasure uh beatin' him tuh death with mah fists." Briggs went on.

Bishop just stared at him for a bit, and took another drink of his whiskey. *"Yer testy, Briggs, an' yer jist like a rat terrier takin' on a pit bull. Yuh bin lucky. Yer speed, an' clever ways has kept yuh from gittin' the stuffins knocked outa yuh, so fur, but I fear yer gonna find out, one uh these times, yuh can't allus be top dog."* Bishop spoke seriously.

"Yuh know Bish, Pa dun tole us, 'it ain't the size uh the dog in the fight, it's the size uh the fight in the dog.'" Briggs laughed, *"Sides I gotta tell yuh, Bish, I done ask a purty woman here in town, tuh marry up with me, an' she tole me she'd be proud tuh. I wants yuh tuh meet her. Bein' mah oldest brother, an' Pa done passed away, I really wants yer blessin'. Yore gonna like her, I know yuh will, an' twould do me proud iffin yuh would give her away, at the hitchin', counta she don't have no kin herebouts 'cept her little girl. She's a widda woman bout mah age. Her husband done wandered off tuh the Yukon tuh dig fer gold, an' done got hisself kilt."* Briggs had an anxious expression on his face as he was telling his brother all this. Bishop came through for him.

"Briggs iffin yuh found yer hearts desire, I wouldn' stand in yer way. Yuh know yer own fortune better than I do. I'd be proud tuh stand at the alter with yuh on yer weddin' day."

Briggs was moved, and at that moment he loved his brother

more than he'd realized at any time in his life. *"Come on, les amble tuh the dinin' hall, an' git us some victuals. Ah'll wager yer bout tuh starve after yer long ride."* He invited.

Bishop drained his glass and answered, *"Yuh know, now thet yuh mention it, yer right, les git to it pronto."*

Briggs left a half dollar on the bartop and they departed the Longbranch together.

Laura looked up in time to see Briggs walk into the dining hall with a stranger. The man was unknown to her, but for some reason he looked vaguely familiar. They sat at a table in the crowded dining hall. Laura hurried to their table.

"Briggs, what can I bring you and yer friend," she smiled at them.

"Laura this here is mah brother Bishop, and Bish this is mah true love Laura."

Bishop got to his feet, and with a courtly bow said, *"Miss Laura I'm proud tuh make yer acquaintance, an' wanna be the first tuh welcome yuh tuh the Clayborn fambily. I wanna say I would be proud tuh stand with you all at the alter whin the time comes."*

Laura blushed, and was delighted with Briggs' brother. *"I'm pleased tuh meet yuh Bishop. We haven't set a date as yet, but it looks like the event will take place in the near future. I'm happy yer included in the weddin', but please let me take yer orders 'fore the boss gits upset."*

Briggs ordered a beefsteak, and fried taters with black coffee, and peach cobbler. Bishop opted for the ham, black eyed peas, and boiled taters, cherry pie, and coffee.

"Whatcha think, Bish?" Briggs asked hopefully.

"Shore is a comely young woman, an' friendly. I kin see she's tookin with yuh the way her eyes lights up whin she talks to yuh. I kin unnerstan how yuh done fell fer the lady, but Briggs duh yuh

know what takin on a ready made fambily kin be like? Maybe the little girl would have a different opinion of yuh than her mom." Bishop shrugged.

"She done tole me already she wants me fer a daddy. She's a purty little thing jest like her mother, an' I believe we kin work it out satisfactory." Briggs clarified.

Laura appeared with their suppers, and placed them on the table.

"Enjoy yore meal, gentlemen," she urged, and left to wait on another customer.

"How do them ladies balance all uh the plates on their arms, an' still walk fast like they do?" Bishop pondered.

"I wager ut's one uh them there mysteries uh life Bish, I don't know." Briggs replied.

They finished their meals, and then Briggs tossed the sack of Bull Durham, and papers across the table to his brother. Bishop rolled himself a neat cigarette, and lit a match on his thumb nail.
Briggs did the same, but scratched his match under the table. He'd busted off a lit match head once, and burned his thumb bad. As the tobacco smoke drifted, each man sat with his own thoughts. Briggs was lost in morass of pale blue eyes, and a musical voice. Bishop had the outlaw, Carmady on his mind, and wondered if ever the 'eye for an eye' vengeance would be carried out. Would the man sent after him be successful?, or would the outlaw foursome overpower, and kill the tracker?
Their thoughts were interrupted by a commotion outside. People were shouting, and running up the street. The brothers glanced at each other, as they arose from the table. Briggs hurriedly dropped a silver dollar by his plate, and they left the dining hall. The towns-people were moving toward Front street, and Briggs discovered why. A mounted, buckskin clad horseman was leading another horse on which a trussed up prisoner was tied to his saddle. It was Carmady, and the hunt had been successful. Bishop turned and stared at his smaller brother.

"Thet's the man yuh were gonna beat tuh death with yer fists? I don't think yer showin' good sense. Tuh me I believe ut's well an' good things turned out as they did. I got faith in yuh Briggs, but thet there looks like too heavy uh load tuh take on."

"Marshal, here's yore prisoner." The deputy tossed the lead rope to Briggs, *"An' I'm sure he's killed again. I found uh dead woman by a campfire, shot through the head, down trail from where I caught up with Carmady."*

Briggs nodded, and led the horse toward the jail. Now that his brother was here he wasn't going to take a chance again on losing Carmady. He was sure he wouldn't have to argue to have one of them in the jail at all times until Monday when the circuit judge would ride in.

Briggs, and Bishop stopped at the jail, and helped Carmady off his horse.

"Kin yuh loosen these ropes, marshal?" he asked hopefully.

"Not on yer life, I won't. Yuh jist march yer hulk in tuh yer cell." Briggs replied.

Carmady looked disgusted, but staggered toward the back where the jail cells stood. Briggs roughly shoved the big man into the cell, and slammed the door.

"Back up tuh the bars, an' I'll cut yer ropes, an' then yuh kin git outa them as best yuh can. I got no more patience with yuh, Carmady." Briggs reached through the bars, and sawed at the ropes holding the man's wrists tightly bound. The last strand parted, and the rope fell to the floor.

"Kick thet there rope outa there so's I kin reach it." he ordered, and Carmady complied, rubbing his wrists, and swinging his arms to restore the circulation.

"Now put yer arms through the bars." Briggs ordered.

The renegade pushed his arms through. Carmady looked

disgusted, but, did as ordered. Briggs put handcuffs on the man's wrists.

"Watch him close Bish, I'm gonna give him uh thorough search. Iffin he even wiggles, gut shoot him!" Briggs' eyes snapped with anger.

Briggs opened the cell door, and stepped inside. He got behind Carmady, and did a through search. All he found was a small two blade pen knife, tobacco, papers, and matches. He carried the items outside the cell, and closed, and locked the door again. He unlocked the handcuffs, and removed them.

"Kin I have mah tobacco, an' papers back?" Carmady asked, without much hope.

"Yup, but I'll take care uh the matches." Briggs answered, tossing the items through the bars.

The outlaw picked up the tobacco, and papers. Then rolled a cigarette. "Hows 'bout a light, an' some food?" He questioned.

Briggs lit a match, and held it outside the bars just within reach of the tip of the cigarette if Carmady pressed his face against the bars.

"Bish, would yuh mind goin' tuh the dining hall, an' gittin' a sandwich, an' some coffee fer our prisoner?" He requested. Bishop turned, and left the jail office. Briggs sat, and waited at the desk.

"Well, lawman I guess yuh won." Carmady admitted. Briggs turned to stare at him. "This ain't no game Carmady. Yuh done kilt mah brother, an' yuh kilt the town marshal, an' iffin whot the deputy says is true, yuh kilt a woman on the trail too. The law can't kill yuh any deader than hangin' yuh once, but tell me, did yuh kill her?" Briggs quizzed the prisoner.

Carmady drew on his cigarette, and blew the smoke through the bars. He stared at the marshal for nearly a full minute.

He didn't think the man was going to answer him, but Carmady shrugged his shoulders, and let them drop in defeat.

"Yeah, I kilt her, too. Done the decent thing though, I let her finish her coffee afor I shot her. Twas a matter uh need. I wanted her outfit, guns, an' horse. Like yuh said law kin only kill me once."

Briggs wished it wasn't so. It was too bad the guilty one couldn't be hung once for each murder he committed.

"Carmady, I hope God has mercy on yer soul, cause I shore don't. I can't find it in mah heart tuh forgive. Yer gonna pay fer yer errors come Monday er Tuesday. Though I don't hold with killin' I swear yuh deserve tuh die at the end of a rope." Briggs told him.

The shadows were gone outside, and dusk was upon them. Briggs lit the lamp, and lowered the chimney. Carmady sat on his cot and didn't offer any more conversation.

Bishop returned to the jail. *"Iffin yuh wanna go romance yer chosen, Briggs, I'll set here, an' watch this low-life fer uh couple uh hours."* He volunteered.

Briggs took him up on the offer, and mounted the horse Carmady had rode in on all trussed up like a turkey. He loped the horse up to Laura's house, and tied him to a tree outside. He rapped on the door, and Laura opened it. She was just as stunning as she had been the first time he fell for her.

Wedding Plans

Chapter 10

"Briggs, do come in." Laura smiled, and held her arms out to him.

He gathered her into his arms, and kissed her. He drew back, and looked into her pale blue eyes.

"Got Carmady in jail again. I hope fer the last time. Mah brother is watchin' him, an' he said 'go romance yer intended'. Not a bad notion, huh?" Briggs grinned, and hugged her.

"Your brother give you some good advice, Briggs. Come set on the couch with me, my love." she urged.

They walked hand in hand, and sat close to each other on the couch. Briggs turned toward her, and placed one arm around her shoulders, and the other about her slim waist. He kissed her tenderly on her soft lips, and Laura eagerly returned his kisses. He left his arm about her shoulders, and related the story of the prisoners' return.

"The circuit judge will be here in a couple uh days, an' then we'll be rid of thet outlaw. We can then carry on with our lives. We kin set a date tuh wed, an' git the preacher tuh marry us Laura. I love yuh more than life itself." he admitted, and knew in his heart there could be no other woman for him.

"Will you come to church with Carrie and me in the morning, Briggs? You can meet the preacher, and we can ask him then if he can marry us next Sunday on the Lord's day. I want us to be a family as soon as we can." Laura appealed to him.

"Shore I will. Bishop won't mind settin' with the prisoner, as I um gonna git back tuh the jail, an' watch him tonight." Briggs agreed. Laura seemed somewhat disappointed.

"I was hoping you would spend the night, and we could consummate our love for each other." She murmured demurely, *"although I was brought up in a Christian home, and believe in the Holy bonds of matrimony, I've been without a husband, and the pleasure*

and closeness a man can provide, for more than a year and a half."

"Laura nothin' would give me greater pleasure, an' lovin' yuh like I do, the offer is more temptin' than I kin resist, but mah conscience wouldn't let me live with muhself. On our weddin' night, mah love, you'll thank me for waitin'" Briggs explained.

"You're right, Briggs. I admire you for the restraint you've shown. You must think me a brazen hussy for suggesting it." Laura was sobered.

"Not in the least. I know mah ownself how powerful the urges kin be, but a man must do whot he must do, an' thet is consider the future of our life together. You, Carrie, an' me." Briggs kissed her, and stood to leave.

"Goodnight, Laura, until the morrow." Briggs took his leave and rode back to the jail.

As he dismounted and wrapped the reins around the rail outside the marshal's office, he thought about what Laura had said. She'd offered herself to prove her love. Briggs had been sorely tempted to give in to his emotions, but his upbringing had overruled. To find she thought that much of him risking the possibility he'd think her a bold wanton. Besides his love for her, he had to admire her struggle to keep herself, and Carrie together as a family, knowing what a difficult task that could be in a man's world. Working six days a week, and still keeping herself appealing was a chore few women would, or even could maintain.

"It's me, Bish." He called as he stepped through the door. *"I made plans tuh go tuh church with Laura, an' talk tuh the preacher 'bout gittin' hitched next Sunday."* Bishop arose from behind the desk.

"Yuh take mah room it the hotel, an' I'll stay here tonight, an' watch Carmady. Yuh come on back by nine o'clock tuh give me time tuh git ready fer church. I'll wanta wash up, an' shave, an' put on some clean clothes. It's room twenty-three, an' there ain't no lock on the door." Briggs told him.

"Yuh git a chance tuh romance with yer intended, Briggs?" Bishop was curious.

"Yeah, we hugged, an' kissed some, an' we done made plans. Thanks again, Bish."

Bishop clapped him on the back as he left the office. He heard his brother ride away, and went to check on his prisoner. Carmady was snoring heavily, and all stretched out on the cot in his cell. There wasn't much else to do until morning. Briggs sat at the desk for a short time, and slowly leafed through the reward posters he found in a lower drawer. He found one with a five hundred dollar reward for some owlhoot named Charlie Goodyear, and one with the name of Woodrow Bascome, but he had no way of knowing these were two of the men that had busted Carmady out of jail. His head began to nod of it's own accord, and he reconed it was neigh time to turn in himself. The cot alongside the west wall of the office looked so inviting, he blew out the lamp, and sat on the edge of the bed. He unbuckled his gunbelt and laid it on the floor.

Slipping his Colt under the pillow, and kicking off his boots, he lay down, and pulled the thin wool blanket over himself. The town of Wolf Point was unusually quiet even for a Saturday night, and Briggs fell asleep hearing a lonesome coyote serenading the half moon riding high in the summer sky.

Briggs awoke with a start later when the moon was low in the western sky. Something had nudged his sense of hearing. He lay waiting for whatever the sound was to be repeated... There it was again! A dry rustle coming from the direction of the jail cells. Was Carmady up to something, or was there someone trying to break him out again? Briggs sat up, and threw the blanket off. He grabbed his six-shooter from under his pillow and stood. The cot creaked with relief and Briggs felt his way toward the cells.

He struck a match, and held it high overhead. It was a packrat dragging a petrified apple core toward it's pile of treasure in one corner of the unused cell. Briggs blew out the match and returned to his cot.

Laura, and her daughter had talked late into the night about the plans for the upcoming wedding. Carrie, naturally wanted to be part of it. Laura promised her she could be maid of honor, and stand with her at the altar when the preacher read the vows. After they had retired, Laura lay awake, and mulled the recent events over, and over in her mind. To have her husband's death verified was, of course, not unexpected, but still it hurt to realize the truth of the matter. Before she had heard, there had been a doubt, and the hope that some day he would indeed return was always in the back of her mind.

On the other hand she was excited with the prospect of her marriage to Briggs whom she had quickly, but deeply fallen in love with. He was the rock solid type of man she could lean on, and share the raising of Carrie with.

She'd been somewhat surprised when her offer of sharing her bed with Briggs had been rejected, but on the other hand she had to admire him even more for his principals. This did nothing, though, for the ache in her heart. Hopefully the ache in her heart would be solved by next week. She finally slept, dreaming about a strong pair of arms around her.

With the dawn came the rain. It was a gentle sprinkle that the earth welcomed, and soaked up quickly. Briggs awoke, and listened to the patter of the drops on the tin roof of the marshal's office. This rain would be a welcome relief from the oppressive heat of the last two days. The steady dripping from the eaves lulled him back to sleep again. Carmady too awoke, and realized he might be seeing his next to the last dawn.

He wondered too how he would spend the last two boring days of his life. He knew justice was quick and they had him dead to rights with the killing of the marshal. Never mind the boy, or the woman on the trail.

He had a twinge of remorse for the woman. She had offered to chase down the horses for him, but he needed her outfit, and she was just in the wrong place at the wrong time.

He wondered why his life had taken a quick turn toward the dark side. It was probably the whiskey. He'd never known his mother, and had been raised by a drunken wreck of a father who had pretty much let him live as best he could. That is when he wasn't being beaten by the old man. The day he rebelled, and had hit his father across the temple with a kerosene lantern was without a doubt the fork in the road of his chance for a normal life. He knew he'd killed him and ran from the law at the tender age of fifteen. He'd lived by his wits from then on, and had become a bounty hunter because he found it was easy money for little work. He too fell back to sleep listening to the raindrops fall on the roof.

Briggs accompanied Laura, and Carrie to the church on Front street later that Sunday morning. He sang the Hymns with his baritone voice and nearly nodded off during the sermon.

They stayed after the service to arrange their marriage for the next Sunday. The minister was happy to oblige, telling them he would announce their plans at the service next Sunday and invite the congregation to remain for the wedding.

Laura, Carrie, and Briggs walked slowly home enjoying the cool day and the smell of rain dampened earth.

"Briggs, may we expect you for dinner?" Laura inquired.

"Sorry, I've gotta git back tuh the jail, an' relieve mah brother. He's gotta git his own dinner, an' take care uh his horse, but iffin yuh cud maybe bring me a bite at the jail, Ah'd be beholdin' tuh yuh." He replied.

"I see no problem with that." Laura smiled, as they arrived at her home, and Carrie skipped ahead to open the door. On the porch Briggs folded Laura in his arms, and planted a passionate kiss on her lips. Laura was surprised, but delighted with his show of affection, and returned his kiss with a vigor that startled him. This woman he loved showed a spark of ardor, and fire, when she nipped his lower lip with her teeth.

"I, Laura, you are a temptress, and iffin mah upbringin' had been different, who knows what I would do. Probably sweep yuh offin yer feet, an' tote yuh tuh yer bed." He admitted. Laura flashed him a wicked smile, and turned to enter the house.

This was a side of Laura he hadn't been aware of. It told him she could be a vixen, as well as a dutiful wife. It gave him a lot to think about on his walk back to the jail. Bishop was happy to see him return.

"Briggs, I'm gonna rustle up some grub. Yuh want me tuh pack some back fer yuh? I will bring somethin' fer the prisoner too." he offered.

Briggs sat down at the desk. *"No, Bish, Laura's gonna bring me some dinner a little later, but I spose yuh cud bring somethin' fer Carmady."*

His brother left the jail to find his lunch, and Briggs entered the cell area to check on Carmady. The big man was sitting on his cot and appeared to be in deep thought.

"Marshal, I'm probably gonna die at the end of a rope in a day er two, an' there's somethin' thet sticks in mah craw. I don't wanna die without knowin iffin I coulda whupped yuh in a rough an' tumble brawl. Yuh claimed yuh cud beat me tuh death with yer fists, an it seems tuh me I'd rather die like thet, than dancin' with a hangman's noose." Carmady told him.

Briggs wasn't really surprised at the man's request, knowing how pride goes before the fall. He'd have to find a way to arrange it.

Laura entered the jail office with a covered platter and watched with pride as Briggs devoured the meal she'd prepared for him. He finished it off with a mug of black coffee. As he leaned back, and smacked his lips with gusto, he complimented Laura on her cooking.

"Laura that was, without a doubt, the best dinner I've enjoyed in mah life!" he sighed.

Laura just glowed with pride. Bishop returned to the jail with some food for the prisoner, and slid it under the cell door.

"Yuh thought 'bout whot I said, marshal?" Carmady inquired.

Bishop turned to his younger brother with a questioning look.

"Carmady wants tuh have a go it it, rough an' tumble. Sez he'd rather die by the fist than the rope, an' I believe I'll oblige. A man must do whot he must do." Briggs shrugged.

"I don't agree, Briggs, an' I suspect yer takin' on more un yuh kin handle, but iffin thet's yer desire I'll not hold yuh back.

Carmady will die fer whot he done. Iffin yuh beat him tuh death, er iffin I have tuh shoot him down, so be it." Bishop soberly told him.

Laura was shocked by Briggs' statement. *"Don't I have a say in this madness? I love you, Briggs, and want a husband. I don't want you to carry through with this. It may not be my place to speak, but I'll take the wrath of your anger rather than see you injured. Men and their foolish pride!"* Her pale blue eyes snapped with anger.

Briggs was chagrined, but determined to give Carmady his chance. Unknown to him Bishop made plans to make sure the fight never took place. He turned, and left the jail to tend to his horse. Later when he saw Laura leave the office, he intercepted her three blocks away. Though she was still in a huff, she greeted him with a smile.

"Miss Laura, don't fret, I'm gonna see to it thet Briggs don't take on thet rowdy. I feel the same as yuh do. He's tryin' tuh tote too heavy uh load, but his pride won't let him back off," he divulged.

"Oh Bishop, I know we're right, and I do thank you, but how are you going to arrange that?" she was puzzled.

"I will be watchin' him after midnight, an' he's gonna be shot while tryin' tuh escape. I ain't got it all worked out yet, but never fret." Bishop tipped his Stetson and took his leave. Laura left with a lighter heart. She had confidence in Briggs' older brother, and was eased by his plan to keep Briggs out of the clutches of the outlaw she was sure would be his downfall.

Briggs sat at the marshal's desk, and whittled a match down to toothpick size to dig for a string of meat caught between his molars.

"Yuh know Carmady even if yuh should win, yer still gonna die when the judge hears yer case. We're gonna hafta do this out behind the jail afore it gits light in the mornin', an' Bishop wull be there holdin' his gun so's yuh don't try tuh run." he advised the outlaw.

"Don't plan on runnin'. I'll stand, an' fight yuh face tuh face like a man." Carmady scowled.

DOUBLE CROSS

Chapter 11

Briggs nodded off sitting in the chair at the desk. From his cot in the cell, Carmady watched him fall asleep and went back to digging at the bars in the cell window with a small, sharp piece of metal he'd been able to conceal in his boot. The mortar was hard on the surface, but crumbly underneath.

He had one of the bars loose at top, and bottom. It wouldn't take much to break it out. The second bar, he had dug out at the top, and was working to loosen the lower end where it was buried in the mortar. This one was proving more difficult, but he kept at it steadily. Briggs shifted in his chair and moaned in his sleep.

Carmady froze at the sound and waited until the marshal was breathing easily again. If he didn't move he was sure the other man couldn't see what he was doing.

He kept digging at the lower end of the bar until it was free, and would turn easily. A sharp blow with the heel of his hand would send both bars flying, and freedom was just a push away.

Unknown to Briggs, his brother, Bishop was on his way to the jail to relieve him. He'd taken a short cut between the buildings, and was coming up behind the marshal's office just as Carmady pushed the two middle bars out, and made his break for freedom.

Bishop heard the noise, and identified where it came from. It could only mean one thing. He stepped back into the shadow of the feed mill, and watched Carmady wriggle out the window. It was strange how fate had a way of upsetting even the best laid of plans, and he smiled, as he realized this was going to solve the part of the plan he had formed, but hadn't resolved as yet.

Carmady had let himself down to the ground and was running right toward the feed mill. Bishop drew his Colt and when Carmady was at point blank range, he fired two quick, but perfectly aimed shots into the running man's chest. In a sense Carmady was free and wouldn't have to worry about a hanging.

Briggs was startled awake by the shots and leapt out of his chair. The shots had come from behind the jail. He rushed out the front door, but was careful as he peeked around the corner of the jail.

"Briggs?" his brother called quietly. *"It's me, Bishop, yer prisoner was escapin'. I was comin' tuh relieve yuh, an' come face tuh face with 'im. I ain't the fighter yuh are, an' it surprised me. I jist drawed, an' fired without thinkin'."*

Briggs lit a match, and looked down at the fallen prisoner. Carmady was lying on his belly. The back of his shirt was crimson with blood. He didn't seem to be breathing, as Briggs struggled to turn him over. There was no doubt about it. The two shots were grouped close together, and could have been covered with a couple of playing cards.

One of the bullets had probably shattered the man's heart. Briggs let the body drop back. He was secretly relieved. Not at all sure he could have beaten the man in a rough, and tumble fight.

"Funny, Bish, how justice is served sometimes. As the Good Book says: 'He who lives by the sword shall die by the six-gun.' Iffin he hadn't bin so quick tuh blow our little brother outa his saddle, er kill the marshal, er the lady on the trail, maybe he coulda lived a decent life."

Bishop grinned. *"Don't believe I ever seen thet in the Bible."*

Some of the curious townspeople were beginning to gather, and one held a lantern up high enough so that the scene was bathed in the eerie glow of the lamplight.

"It's all over folks. Carmady has done paid the price uh his misdeeds. Yuh kin see there where he done dug away at the bars until he could wriggle out. Bishop here done cashed 'im in, so I guess it'll be boothill fer him in the mornin'" Briggs explained. Most of the muttering heard was either *'good riddance'* or, *'I wanted tuh see a hangin.'*

The next morning Carmady's body was dumped in an unmarked grave on boot hill, and unceremoniously covered with dirt. The week passed slowly for Briggs, but at last Sunday was at hand. Following the sermon, the minister did indeed marry him and his love Laura. Carrie got her wish and was allowed to stand at her mother's side at the altar. When Briggs was ordered to kiss the bride, she nipped him on the lower lip again. It promised to be a wedding night he would never forget.

Printed in the USA
CPSIA information can be obtained
at www.ICGtesting.com
JSHW082340140824
68134JS00020B/1783